"Brigid, Brigid. Shhh." Her fingers caressed my arm. "Of course you're upset. God knows. I remember how I felt the first time."

"What in the hell are you talking about?" But my anger was dying, murdered by the gentle strokes of her hand.

"Gen has taken off before."

"You think she just left?" I was incredulous. "Where'd the blood come from?"

"I don't know. The first time it wasn't blood. It was ketchup."

"That's blood up there on her pillow."

"Yes. It is. The second time, it was menstrual blood."

She looked terrible, deeply troubled, deciding between evils I could not even imagine. "The third time . . . It's happened three times . . . The third time . . ." The pause was long as she gathered strength from somewhere, perhaps from me. Her hand lay motionless now on mine. "The third time . . ."

She couldn't seem to get past it. I said, brisk and jarring, "The third time what?"

"She got the blood from a neighbor."

"From a neighbor?" A collage of vampires and crosses in a foggy Carpathian twilight filled my mind.

Through her hand lying on my wrist I felt Pat's shudder. Her fingers trembled the way an aspen trembles in the wind before a storm.

About the Author

Karen lives in a little yellow house, a former one room school house, in a meadow where Holsteins graze in summer. She lives there with a dog named Sam, who walks her in the morning and in the evening after work, and with a cat named Kiki, who keeps her on her toes. For work, Karen organizes women who are on welfare, and she also runs a small experimental college program for rural low income people in Downeast Maine. For fun, she gardens and looks forward to fishing again someday in the pond across the road. Keeping good rural hours, Karen gets up at four and writes three hours every morning. Her friends say they wouldn't mind this so much if she didn't always fall asleep at eight o'clock at night.

Murder
IS RELATIVE

Karen Saum

The Naiad Press, Inc.
1990

Printed in the United States of America
First Edition

Edited by Katherine V. Forrest
Cover design by Pat Tong and Bonnie Liss
    (Phoenix Graphics)
Typeset by Sandi Stancil

Library of Congress Cataloging-in-Publication Data

Saum, Karen, 1945—
    Murder is relative / by Karen Saum.
        p.   cm.
    ISBN 0-941483-70-3
    I. Title.
PS3569.A7887M87   1990
813'.54--dc20   90-6134
                                                            CIP

*To Louise Saum
and to the memory of
Jack Saum.
Their love and support
made Brigid Donovan possible.*

Chapter 1

It was too late, I had decided, to call Claire Du
Lac Tuesday night when I arrived, so I drove directly
to the hotel on Place Terrasse Dufferin overlooking
the St. Lawrence River. I used the Chateau Frontenac
to guide me. It was only 8:00 p.m. and still light, but
I was tired and I wanted to walk around the old
walled city before I went to bed. It had been ten
years or more since I had visited Quebec. I reasoned
that being eighty or so, Claire Du Lac would prefer
not to hear from me until morning. That's the kind

1

of reasoning I've been trying to undo, ever since my last drunk a few twenty-four hours ago.

"How much did Ed tell you?" she asked after gently chiding me for not having called when I arrived. "I waited up until midnight," she reproved.

The parlor where we sat was turn-of-the-century. So was she. The chairs and the sofa were covered in a deep red plush, lace antimacassars on the arms and headrest; she wore a crocheted shawl, her hair grey and thin and pulled tightly into a bun set low on her skull. Jesus bled on a big brass crucifix above her and in a picture on the mantel he pointed delicately at his bleeding heart. She spoke with an accent.

"Not much," I said. He hadn't. When he called the day before yesterday I knew he was drunk: it was already noon.

"Would you like some coffee?" Claire Du Lac asked.

The windows were hung with heavy lace curtains; the Persian carpet, in the dim light, glowed like dying embers. On a table beside the glass-fronted bookcase a plaster Pietà seemed somberly radiant. Her eyes were small and bright in a face delicately boned, skin like parchment.

"No," I decided. "Thanks. Ed said something about your wanting a history of your . . ." I groped for words, staring at the crucifix over her head. "Your faith?" I tried.

For a moment she looked at me blankly. "No. Of H.O.P.E. You never heard about it?" She picked up a brochure from a pile on the table beside her. "Look at this," she commanded.

H.O.P.E. it said, and then in smaller letters, "Helping Others, the Poor Especially."

2

"Established in nineteen sixty-five by an interfaith group sponsored by the Maine Council of Churches, H.O.P.E. brings together people from many diverse faith commitments from Bahai to Roman Catholic, from Zen Buddhist to Islam, all united in their desire to alleviate human suffering in whatever form it appears."

The rest of the brochure contained pictures and captions. I nodded, said, "It's interesting," and tried to hand it back to her.

"No, no. You keep it. I have more."

"What is it you want me to do?"

"Write about it," she said promptly. "It's a wonderful organization. H.O.P.E. Even the name. My late husband served on the board and since his passing I try to help. These brochures are my project." She looked down at them modestly. "Now I think a book. I hope Ed is interested, but . . ."

She shrugged, making of her right hand a bottle, tipping it to her lips. She looked at me inquiringly. "But not you. Or at least not any more."

I decided her eyes were bright for a reason. "No," I admitted. "Not anymore."

"You are interested then?"

"Tell me more about it," I conceded.

"Not much to tell. I think just to write the history, how it grows, the people it helps. Describe it."

"Your husband?"

"Oh certainly. But not for that reason. Not . . ." She paused. "No eulogy."

I thought a minute. "How long?" I asked.

"I don't think it takes more than six months."

"No. I meant the book."

"Two, three hundred pages. I think that is enough. I must approve it. And the H.O.P.E. board. You and I, we must consult as it comes."

"And the pay?"

"Five thousand dollars plus expenses." Then she added, "American."

Even so. My expression must have told my disappointment.

"Room and board are part of expenses. And mileage, of course. And secretary."

I nodded. "The living allowance. How much is it?"

"Not allowance," she replied. "Room and board. You will live at the community. I pay them direct."

She raised her finger to check my protest. "I assure you, you won't regret nothing. You work for H.O.P.E. and they have, what do you say, a cap on salaries. They say, 'Live simply so others can simply live.' "

I studied some red and blue glass anemones in a vase by my side. On their stamens were tiny globules of gold. On the petal of one a small diamond raindrop burned in a sudden shaft of sunlight.

I asked, "What about when it's published?"

"H.O.P.E. holds the copyright and receives royalties."

She seemed to sense she had lost me. "I am willing, on publication, to pay you five thousand more."

I went back to figuring. My bank statement last month showed only forty-eight dollars over the minimum balance. By next month, if something didn't break, I'd be living on plastic. "How much for travel?"

4

"They pay fifteen cents a mile."

I started to get up.

"Wait!" The restraining hand she laid on mine was small and dry and hooked like the claw of a bird. "How about I give you a hundred a month for travel?"

"A hundred fifty plus fifteen cents a mile," I countered.

"Done!" she said. "You get a hundred fifty direct from me. But," she continued, "you must not mention this arrangement to anyone there. Now . . ."

In the pause that followed I had a sickening presentiment I had sold my soul for pottage.

"There is one more thing," she continued. "Ed tells me you do investigative journalism." She nodded at a pile of several books lying on the sofa. I recognized for the first time the dust jacket of the book on top. It was one of mine, one I'd done on a murder committed some fifty years before on a plantation in Aroostook County, Maine. The murder had not been solved when I undertook to write about it, having been intrigued by the story which my landlady in Greenville had told me. "I know who did it," she had confided one night. It was January. We had cabin fever, she and I. Bit by bit she recounted the long dead passions that had led, in her youth, to that ultimate crime, murder. That same winter, in February, I inherited a little money, enough to keep me for a year or so if I was careful, and I am. I decided to write a book about it. My researches led to a belated trial and a conviction. My landlady had been right, she had known, but for all the wrong reasons.

"Yes," I allowed. "I do."

"My son-in-law he was murdered." Her voice, thin and reedy, cracked. "In Surry, near H.O.P.E. Just last week." She turned her head from me. Her fingers twisted her handkerchief into a knot.

I waited.

"I'm frightened," she offered finally, her voice tentative, her manner an invitation for help. There was a time, and not too long ago, when I would have responded. No more. I waited.

"If you happen to find out anything about it . . ." She faltered again, her eyes seeking mine. "Well, please let me know."

"How much?" I asked.

"Whatever you find out. I am interested."

"No. How much will you pay?"

She looked at me shrewdly. "Ed tells me you are very sharp. I must look out. That is good. I don't mind."

We sat a while in silence. I should probably have gone. But the thought of investigating another murder had me hooked. I think by this time Claire Du Lac had me hooked. That she had provided me with a cover to investigate her son-in-law's murder excited me. I had rapidly taken it as a fact that the history of H.O.P.E. was a cover she had devised. It would take much longer for me to realize that the murder investigation was a cover too.

"Five hundred," she said finally. "Five hundred a week. American."

I stopped in Greenville to pick up some things. Nell, my landlady, was dismayed to hear that this job would keep me away most of the summer at least. Not, she assured me, that she minded for herself.

There'd be, she said, oodles of folk tickled pink to do the things we'd planned to do together: go fishing, a week at Chesuncook, camping in the Laurentides. No, it was for me she was concerned, traipsing off to the coast — at my age. Fifty-two to her seventy-four, but, except for her motherly bullying, it's true she seemed the younger — splitting the stove wood, felling trees, staying up half the night after meetings telling tales and having fun.

"Out and around with that drunk and not going to meetings."

She meant Ed, who had put me in touch with Claire Du Lac. Ed makes her nervous. Truth is, Ed makes me nervous. But old habits die hard, bad ones especially. Ed is the last of my bad old habits. A few twenty-four hours ago, he was my drinking buddy of last resort. Depending on my mood, I justify seeing him in one of three ways. Goody-Two-Shoes: "I'm going to reform the old reprobate. Poor-me's: Ed loves me even if no one else does. Proud, as in before a fall: who me take a drink? Nell says, "You go visit Ed and don't think for one minute you're coming back here stinking drunk." I reassured her. I promised to come home every Friday night to take her to our favorite meeting. The Moosehead Lake Group, right there in Greenville.

She sniffed, mollified, having got what she wanted. And then a final skirmish, her parting blow, a love tap. "What about your kids?"

Not fair. Distinctly below the belt. My kids, as she called them, were both grown up, quite able to take care of themselves. God knows they'd had to most of their lives. "Yeah," I encouraged, "what about my kids?"

"Don't get huffy. They just *might* want to come for a visit."

"Get off my case, Nell. Are you saying if I'm not here, they're not welcome?" That I knew was a crock. I sometimes think the only reason Nell puts up with me all winter long is so she can have the twins to play with on occasion in the summer.

"Brigid, you're impossible sometimes. It's *you* they come to see."

The twins are twenty-nine and thirty. They look a lot alike and they had once been inseparable, clinging to each other during the hard years of growing up. Hard for them, hard for me. I didn't find AA until they were adults. Their dad walked out on us when Johnny was born. That wasn't supposed to happen to us who came of age in the fifties. Nor was falling in love with women supposed to happen. But that I started to do when I was twelve. Mother called them crushes. She called them growing pains. At seventeen, I mistook my passion for Sr. Anne, our American history teacher, not for a growing pain but for a vocation. In the convent, which I entered out of high school, another novice, Beth, clarified my mistake, and Mother's. In the midst of this clarification, our Formation Director suggested that Beth's was not a true vocation; I concluded that mine wasn't either. I seemed to have gotten pregnant on my first night out, a date Mother fixed up for me. I say seemed to; I don't remember. But it wasn't parthenogenesis that produced little Danny. I stayed sober during my pregnancy; alcohol made me puke. How I knew Johnny was on the way, two months after Danny arrived, was I started upchucking my martinis again. When the twins' Dad left, the jug and I were reunited, a condition of friendship to which I was constant for twenty years.

Not wasting time on a derisory look, I said to Nell, "See you Friday."

The drive from Greenville to the coast of Maine takes only a couple of hours, but it's like going through a time warp. Up north there's just the woods and mountains with every fifteen minutes or so a cluster of white frame houses with stately elms and maples bordering the highway. Then come two nineteenth-century milltowns, villages really, Guilford and Dover-Foxcroft. Dover-Foxcroft, closer to civilization and the 1990s, has a boutique on Main Street and a health food restaurant with a Boston fern hanging on the porch summers. But it's not enough to prepare you for Bangor, the sudden flatness, and Broadway as it comes honky-tonk out of town. Anywhere, U.S.A., McDonalds to the left of you, Burger King on the right.

Surry, where H.O.P.E. is situated, is a hamlet on Patten Bay. H.O.P.E. itself, nestled between blueberry barren and bog, some five miles out of town, looks Currier and Ives, a cluster of clapboard and shingled houses with split rail fencing surrounding the pastures. A horse-drawn sled, repaired and painted, stood beside the wooden sign: Welcome to H.O.P.E.

Interfaith it might have been, but the first several people I met turned out to be Catholic Sisters. None of them wore habits. There was, I discovered a few days later, a convent of sorts down the road where a cloistered and habited order of Sisters lived. But those at H.O.P.E., like me, wore jeans and flannel shirts and blue bandannas on their greying heads.

9

Accommodations, my cell, as I thought of it, was a tiny cabin, about eight by ten. It smelled fresh, like Pine-Sol. Furnishings were an iron cot, a desk small but sturdy, and a chest of drawers. Two hooks on the back of the door held two hangers which rattled until I draped my raincoat on one and a jacket on the other. The window, above the desk, looked out on a pasture where a very pregnant Holstein browsed. I tested the bed and thought it would do. The only light was an overhead one. I'd have to find a table lamp. I took out my AA meeting book and decided to try the one in Blue Hill that night. OD, Open Discussion. Shouldn't be too heavy. First I'd give Ed a call.

"There's an open meeting tonight in Blue Hill," I said, twelfth-stepping him for the three millionth time. In AA we have a 12-step program of recovery. The twelfth step is carrying the message to others suffering from alcoholism.

"Sure and there's an unopened bottle of Jamison's with your name on it I been saving all these lonely years," replied Ed.

"I want to talk with you. When you're sober."

"And aren't I always sober, darlin' Brigid?"

I dropped by after the meeting to touch base with him. Nothing more. Ed had once been a reporter for the *New York Times*. In a profession that seems to breed alcoholism, Ed Kelly's courtship and affair with the bottle was nothing remarkable; his business sense, perhaps, once was. He retired fifteen years ago to manage some property he'd picked up for a song in Blue Hill, Maine, during the fifties. On Blue Hill Bay, the three elegant Victorian houses, had he remodelled them into condos, would have been worth a million each. But, "Not before I'm dead," he would say, "will these lovely ladies be turned into tarts." He lived on the second floor of one of them and enjoyed a comfortable income renting the other five apartments. In my boozing days, Ed and I had slept off many drinking bouts together. He seemed to have regarded this practice as an affair. Who knows. Maybe it was. I don't remember. Whatever, it hadn't affected our friendship. My sobriety had. We really didn't see much of each other anymore.

He didn't seem surprised to hear I was investigating the murder of David Thorne, Grandmère (Gram) Du Lac's son-in-law. We sat in his study with its book-lined walls and out-sized roll-top desk spilling papers and pamphlets. Books open and closed lay about on the floor and on the furniture.

"Don't mind the mess," he said perfunctorily, waving his hand at it. He was, he said, writing a history of the Cajun Diaspora, which took place in these parts in 1755. He also wrote for the weekly *Blue Hill Packet*.

"Tell me about it," I invited.

"The Diaspora?" He looked puzzled.

"The murder, Ed."

"Be careful of her, Brigid."

"Du Lac?" I asked, but I wasn't really surprised. "Why's that?"

"Don't get me wrong. She's a grand old lady. Are you sure I can't get you a drink? No. Well, then. What was I saying now?"

"She's a grand old lady."

"Sure. And she is. But crooked as a corkscrew. Not straight. If you get my drift."

I didn't. But I filed it away to pursue in the morning when Ed comes as close to sobriety as he gets. It had puzzled me, once the initial elation subsided, why she wanted me to look into Thorne's death. "I'm frightened," she had said. I doubted Lucifer would frighten her much.

All I got from Ed that first evening was a name, Edith Wardwell and information I had already read in the *Packet*. He probably had written the article. David Thorne, age 56, had been bludgeoned to death at the Thorne's summer cottage. His body had not been discovered until at least twenty-four hours later. Jerry Grindle, a local man who did maintenance for summer folk, found him. Thorne's wife, Angele, had been in Quebec City visiting her mother, Claire Du Lac, formerly of Mount Desert Island, at the time of the murder. Prostrated by grief — at this Ed winked — she had no idea who might have done such a terrible thing. The murder weapon, found by the body, was a hammer. Whoever had committed the crime had apparently worn gloves. The police had no leads, and, Ed assured me owlishly, never would have any.

"And Claire Du Lac's interest. What is it? To see justice done?" I probed.

"Brigid, Brigid," he admonished, "you mustn't think just because . . ." and then he began to snore. I took my tea cup to the kitchen sink before I left.

12

Chapter 2

The next morning I learned that David Thorne had been a member of "the club."

"You coming to the memorial for David T. tonight, Sister?" the young man at the grocery store asked, shyly. He had been at the AA meeting the night before. His name was Peter.

His bright eyes looked inquiring, looked deferential. My heart surprised me. I somehow didn't want to give it up. I tried momentum to maintain my determination. "You mustn't," I rushed on, "call me Sister, you see . . ."

He looked stricken. "I didn't think," he began. Then, "But it's okay. I mean, it's not like you're the first . . ." The blush rose to his eyes bringing the sheen of tears.

In my need to rescue him it never occurred to me to say, "Hey! I'm not a nun." Instead I lightly reassured him with, "Don't sweat it!"

I wondered which of the nuns I would find at future meetings. And I shared Peter's misgivings for having broken the AA pledge of anonymity. I chided him by paraphrasing it: "What you see there, what you hear there, when you leave there, let it stay there."

"I know. I'm really sorry," he said.

Out in the sunshine I realized I had straightened out nothing. He still thought I was a nun. "None of this and none of that," the boys at St. Andrews High School used to say.

I spent the rest of Thursday morning getting the feel of H.O.P.E. My impression was that Congregationalists administered it, Sisters monopolized social services, Buddhists managed the craft workshops, and a group of aging hippies controlled the People's Building, the name they had given the auditorium where, of all things, they put on operas twice a year. Mrs. Gross, the general manager, suggested a visit with Edith Wardwell.

"Edith," she said, "has been with us from the beginning. She's retired now and lives in that little cottage by the main gate. Edith *is* H.O.P.E. I realize you'll want to do your own research, but, believe me, you could, if you wanted, just ghost the story from what she tells you. As a matter of fact, when Mrs. Du Lac approached us to do this history, that's what I suggested."

Edith, as she insisted I call her, was expecting me. There was a tentative quality to her that reminded me of my mother, reminded me of many small women. It was, perhaps a remnant of some survival technique, an instinct to expose the jugular when the odds seemed overwhelming. A tenderness with the tensile strength of a spider's web.

"I didn't know but whether you might like something to drink?" She raised a fruit glass, half full, the liquid in it amber, reminiscent of Ed's unopened bottle of Jamison's. I wondered for a giddy moment whether she and Ed were in cahoots to get me drunk.

"It's apple juice," she said dryly, and I thought of Claire Du Lac and her canniness. "But I also have tea and coffee. Nothing stronger I'm afraid."

"Apple juice would be fine."

"In the fridge. The glasses are in the cupboard to the left of the sink, as you face it."

I noticed for the first time that the chair she sat in was a wheelchair.

"Arthritis," she explained. "It's just easier if I can roll around. I can walk if I need to."

There wasn't much space for rolling around. The room served every purpose except for bathing. A day bed and a small weaving frame shared one wall; sink, stove and refrigerator another. She sat at a trestle table, facing a sewing machine. Behind her, french doors opened onto a screen porch overlooking the pasture and the pregnant Holstein cow.

"It's got everything I need," she said, acknowledging my inspection. I poured my apple juice. "You can just put those magazines on the floor if you want to take notes," she suggested, gesturing at the clutter along the table top.

Her hair, perfectly white, was soft about her face. She wore a cotton house dress and a pink cardigan. I never knew my grandmother, but Edith Wardwell reminded me of her, right down to the faint pink blush of her gentle, wrinkled cheek. I thought maybe I was falling in love.

"What can I do for you?" she asked when I was settled.

"You know about the history."

"Oh yes. I know about the history." There was something, was it rueful, in her tone. It took a lot of energy for me to say nothing, especially after a minute passed in silence.

"There is Sid," she said abruptly. It sounded as if I was meant to infer something like "In the beginning . . ."

On the clean first page of my notebook I wrote "Sid."

"No, no," she corrected. "There. At the gate. Would you mind going out and calling him for me. Tell him Edith would like to see him for just a minute."

Sid was tall and blond and would have been handsome except for the look in his eyes, like a startled horse, and the scruffiness of him, of his hair and his clothes. When I called to him he stopped, but did not turn. I delivered my message to his back. He never did look at me.

I said, "Edith would like to see you. She said it would only take a minute."

Head averted, he nodded and trudged back to the cottage. I waited until he reemerged before I went back in.

"Everything okay?" I asked, but Sid paid no attention to me. His age was hard to tell. Anywhere from twenty to forty it might have been.

"Thank you," said Edith as I resumed my seat. "Now you've met Sid."

"Sort of."

She laughed. "He's funny," she admitted. "He either takes to you or he doesn't. Now what would you like to know from me?"

I confided to her Mrs. Gross's suggestion that I simply ghost the story as told by Edith Wardwell. Edith laughed, pleased. "I suspect, however, that wouldn't satisfy Gram."

"Gram?"

"Du Lac. We call her Gram. Knew her before she got all that money. Used to be dirt poor like the rest of us."

"Oh." I remembered the rug, the carved mahogany breakfront and chaise, the jeweled anemones. "It doesn't seem like new money," I ventured.

"She and Jean got the furnishings too. Of the cottage. You don't know anything about it, do you?" she asked.

"No."

"Well." Edith paused, putting the tips of her fingers together and contemplating them for a while.

17

She sighed and continued. "Well, she knew you weren't going to write a history of H.O.P.E. without talking to me, so she must want me to tell you what I know and that includes what I know about her. And that's more'n'd fill a thimble. That's for sure."

It turned out to be more than would fill a tub.

I dislike the hypocrisy of a gossip who justifies by saying, "it's the truth, it's not gossip." If it's the truth, it's not slander, but it's still gossip. Edith was no hypocrite. "Now there's a lot who would call this gossip," she declared. "But I say — and mind, I'm no women's libber — if it's a woman says it, it's called gossip. But if it's a man, then it's rumors. Well, rumors or gossip, it's the truth. I've known the Du Lacs pretty near all my life. She and Jean moved to the Island my senior year in high school. They came from Quebec somewhere. Lived down the road from us. Not much older, and we got to be friends. Not intimate, but good neighbors.

"He worked some in the woods. Gone all winter the first few years. Up in the lumber camps on the Allagash. Claire didn't like that much, especially after Angele was born. Didn't have food stamps and all that stuff back then. Surplus food's all and not much of that. When you were hungry, you were hungry, period. Claire, now, was nothing if not strong-willed. So she went and got a job for him, caretaking. That would have been in thirty-seven, before the war. Good job, good pay, and secure. They weren't the Rockefellers, the folks they worked for, but might as well have been.

"When the old man died in sixty-eight, he left Jean and Claire some property, no more'n a hundred acres, but shore front, and the guest house there on the bay, furnished and all. It was part of the MDI estate. Not the whole thing, but what you might call the choicest part of it. Ten years later, when Jean died, Claire sold it, for a lot. A million at least. It's a motel and restaurant there now."

The child, Angele, had grown up on the estate on Mount Desert Island. The wealthy owners, who were childless, treated her like their own. Each summer they invited flocks of young folk, nieces and nephews, children of friends, turning their estate into a watering spot for the scions of Park Avenue. Angele married one of them. David Thorne.

Edith proved to be less forthcoming on the subject of Angele and David Thorne.

I asked, "Did Angele and David live on Mt. Desert Island after their marriage?"

"No."

"Where did they live?" I tried.

"David was from New York."

"Oh," said I. "They lived in the city."

"They had a house there," she admitted.

I reflected on her distinction between gossip and rumor and between those and slander. Was Edith's diffidence, I wondered, due to nice feelings, or was some scandal attached to the young couple?

Edith began to talk, this time on a topic of her choosing. "Angele's father, Jean Du Lac, was very generous to H.O.P.E. Those first few years, if it hadn't been for him, I doubt we would have survived. But he was always there with the do-re-mi when we needed it. Yours truly saw to that."

I stopped taking notes, not interested in Jean Du Lac and his musical money. I wanted to learn more about the dead David Thorne and his consort Angele, wanted to break down Edith's resistance to my questions.

"Look," said Edith, responding to my unspoken frustration, "I think I'm talking over your head. I think maybe you should do some homework on H.O.P.E. When Lois, that's Lois Gross, the general manager, when she told me you were coming, I had her bring me a file of our old newspapers. Why don't you read through those. That will keep you busy for a while. And out of mischief. When you're done, say tomorrow afternoon, come on back. You'll know better what you're doing and how I can help. The newspapers are in that shopping bag by the door."

I find it hard to resist dismissals, and I could hardly pretend that this wasn't one. I strove for insouciance, which I've noticed and admired in others. I said, "David Thorne was murdered last week."

"I can't imagine what that can possibly have to do with the history of H.O.P.E.," said Edith, her voice not tender at all. "If it's rumors you're after, I've an old acquaintance with a storehouse full. And there you'll get something stronger to drink than apple juice. Ed Kelly. He lives in Blue Hill. Writes for the *Packet*."

There was so much I wanted to deny: gossip, drunkenness, generally unprofessional behavior. It wasn't until later, honing my mortification by reviewing the scene, that I noticed the laughter. Edith Wardwell, I suspected, had been putting me on. I was almost sure of it. Ed Kelly had sent me to her and she, damn her, had sent me right back again. I felt like a shuttlecock.

* * * * *

20

"Well, did you meet him?" Ed asked after pressing me, routinely, to accept "my" bottle of Jamison's. It was mid-afternoon. I had already done my homework, read most of the newspapers Edith had given me.

"Meet whom?" I asked, knowing suddenly.

"Sid."

"As a matter of fact I did, why?"

"He's Edith's pet. Just wondered what you thought of him."

"Not a whole lot. I didn't talk with him or anything. Just saw him. As a matter of fact he wouldn't even look at me. What's his problem?"

"Drugs," said Ed promptly.

We sat in a bow window overlooking Blue Hill Bay. In close, a fishing boat had stopped among a cluster of lobster buoys. A young man with a pony tail began to haul in a trap. Beyond him the bay was flecked with sails. My day's labors must have put me in a philosophic mood. I found ironic the contrast between the native working in his battered boat and the people from away playing in their expensive toys. I mentioned it to Ed.

"Don't be sentimental, Brigid," he said. "That young man with the pony tail is probably not from these parts either. No more'n you or me."

Not content with my silence, Ed prodded. "Think of yourself, Brigid. How many shit jobs have you taken since you've been in Maine? To get by. To get back to the land. To buy booze. To write your novel. Jobs people with no skills would have had before the likes of yourself came like a plague of locusts to devour their fair land."

Plenty. The answer was plenty. One summer a

21

couple of us even picked the Gardiner dump for copper wire and, in the process, drove into destitution a family that had been eking out a meager living there. We had, until Ed opened our eyes, been proud of our willingness to work so hard for so very little.

I remained silent, being too diffident to retaliate by noting how the indigenous people had been dispossessed of their land and their homes by people from away who, like carpetbaggers, came and drove up real estate prices and real estate taxes in a spiral of inflation no native except the well-off could withstand.

"I don't mean to say I'm entirely innocent," Ed conceded, spinning the ice in his depleted highball. "But God knows I've spent more money here than ever I took away."

Big deal, I thought, seeing how he probably spent all of it on the likes of me to clean his houses and to paint and renovate them. I wondered if he thought his booze was from a local moonshiner. Vodka from the Allagash. Boondock Bourbon. I thought I better leave or I'd be claiming my bottle of Jamison's.

"I don't mean to be hard on you, Brigid. In your way, you were innocent too. But there's others weren't innocent at all. Not by a long shot. You asked about Sid. A case in point. A case of rape."

"Sid was raped?" For some reason the thought was more shocking to me than if he had been a woman.

"Are you daft?" Ed snorted. "His mother. Sixteen she was. The kid was never right. Took to drugs when he was no more'n knee high to a grasshopper.

22

Ended up in the Bangor Funny Farm. Would be there still if it hadn't been for H.O.P.E. and for Edith."

I thought about it for a while. "Someone from away?" I asked.

He didn't answer. He seemed to be calculating. He looked through the watery remnants of his drink at the sunshine bright on the bay. Calculating the drinks he had had, or the drink he was going to have. There was a time at the beginning when I couldn't bear to calculate all the drinks I was denying myself in the bleak dry years ahead. Until someone at a meeting once said to me, "But you're not, you see. There's only one drink you've got to give up. The next one. That's all. Just one."

For some reason it had helped. I figured I could handle one, my higher power and me. Together we could manage one.

"Yes. Someone from away," Ed said. "That's the rumor," he added, quite seriously. I burst out laughing. "I don't see the humor in it," he said huffily and got up to pour himself another drink. When he did, I said good-bye.

David Thorne must have been good people. He was sincerely eulogized at the memorial, by all kinds, native and from away, old timers, and, weeping, some newly sober. I asked Peter, my young friend from the grocery store, to point out David's wife to me. He looked at me in surprise and then said brusquely, "She's not here."

23

Well, it was I who had insisted we observe anonymity. Much of the rest of the meeting my mind wandered, wondering how I might get Edith to gossip. I thought she'd get a kick out of Ed's rumors. I was in for a surprise.

Chapter 3

"Ed told me a rumor," I confided to Edith the next morning.

"What was that?" she asked, smiling.

There was something different about Edith I couldn't put my finger on. I thought it might have something to do with the way she smiled. And I realized that yesterday she hadn't smiled at all. Not once. "You're feeling better today," I said abruptly.

She nodded. "High pressure," she said.

I must have looked puzzled for, with a touch of

yesterday's asperity, she explained, "The arthritis. It's a barometer."

"Oh," I said, and thought, how awful.

"So what was Ed's rumor?"

"About Sid."

Her eyes, which had been friendly and amused became guarded. "What about him?" her voice as full of burrs as a sheep dog's coat.

"Ed was giving me a hard time —"

"So what's new?"

"Oh." Somehow I'd always thought of Ed's bullying as something he did just with me. It was oddly shocking to find it was only his personality. Like discovering he was unfaithful.

"Well," I continued, subdued, "he was badgering me for being from away and taking . . ." I groped for a sanitized adjective. "Poor paying jobs," I managed.

"Shit jobs," Edith corrected, her good humor restored. "I've forgotten more four letter words than you'll ever know. My daddy was a Navy man."

We laughed in a companionable way. "Have another cup of coffee," she suggested. I poured us each a cup. We had discovered we both liked our coffee black, could bear it with milk, and that it surpassed our combined understanding how anyone could like it with sugar alone. "Let's sit out on the porch," she suggested. I opened the french doors and rolled her out. The air was fresh, washed by an early morning shower, and scented with the smell of lilacs and fresh-cut grass. A lawn mower hummed faintly in the distance.

"Sid's at work," Edith said, then explained: "The lawn mower. Sometimes he forgets. But that's him.

26

Sounds like he's mowing behind Woodworking. Now you were telling me about Ed's rumor."

"Right. Well he was hassling me about taking shit jobs like this . . ." And I rattled off a few that had seen me through lean times. Slinging hash at the Waco Diner in Eastport was one.

"When were you at the Waco Diner?" she asked.

"Spring of seventy-eight."

"You must know Olive LaPlante."

"Olive! Sure I know Olive. Stayed with her as a matter of fact, until I found a room. How do you know Olive?"

"We're sisters."

"Oh yeah?" Olive had been good to me, had wanted me to stay on with her, rent free, no problem. No problem for her perhaps.

But she was forever twelfth-stepping me, trying to take me to a meeting, to make me sober:

"There's an open meeting down to Machias tonight, wanna come?"

"This speaker's meeting in Calais is really terrific. I think you'd like it."

But my kids had only just grown up, had only just gone off to school, were on their own. No more having to worry about getting a meal on the table for them by six o'clock, or shopping after work, ironing after dinner. I was ready to get down to some serious boozing, some boozing I could really enjoy.

It never happened. I made the mistake of taking Olive up on her first AA invitation. For the hell of it, for voyeurism, to see the drunks. I thought it might be good material for a novel and I took my notebook along. It was a few twenty-four hours before I picked

27

up my own white newcomer's chip at a meeting in Fairfield, but I never enjoyed a drink or a drunk after that one meeting with Olive in Eastport.

"Tell her I'm sober," I said.

"She knows."

It took me a minute to catch all the implications. Then I asked, "How is she?"

"Good. Says to tell you to bring me up some weekend. Says to tell you that the Eastport meeting Saturday night is good as it ever was."

"Awright!"

"Anyway. Back to your shit jobs. What do they have to do with Sid?"

"Oh. Just that some people from away are worse'n me."

"Oh really! I'm glad Ed noticed that," she said wryly.

"Yeah. Well. He said Sid's mother was raped. When she was sixteen, and that Sid never was quite right. Said he'd been in the Bangor Mental Health Institute before he came here."

In the long silence that followed I feared I might have undone the fragile ties of friendship that had begun to form through my knowing Olive.

"He said," I added, after a while, "that if it hadn't been for you and H.O.P.E. there's no telling what would have happened to Sid."

"Does he know who Sid's father is?" she asked.

"He didn't say," I replied.

"Find out!" she instructed.

It was too early in the morning and I was too sleepy to find that odd.

Driving to Greenville later that afternoon, I reflected that Edith's interest in my history of

28

H.O.P.E. had been perfunctory. "I read the newspapers," I had told her as we drifted, for the most part silent, in a drowsy summer haze.

"Mmm hmm," she had responded.

I had had some questions jotted down to ask her. But my notebook, inside the house, seemed a long way away, so I let it ride. Time enough on Monday I had thought.

On Monday I would have to see Ed. Find out what, if anything, he knew about Sid's father. It wasn't until the drive to Greenville that I realized once again that I was marching to Edith's orders. That only once had I brought up David Thorne's murder, and then Edith had avoided answering me.

"I was surprised," I had said, along about mid-day, "that David Thorne's widow wasn't at the memorial service last night."

Edith had snorted. "Ask your friend Ed to explain that one," she advised.

Together it wouldn't make much of a report for Claire Du Lac whom I was to see Saturday afternoon. But I'd been on the case only two days, I reassured myself, justifying myself to the old woman who appeared vividly in my mind, sharp with condemnation, reminding me how much she had been willing to pay me, for what, for some gossip? Gossip she could have told me herself.

My mental projection of Claire Du Lac's reprimand had me feeling defensive, on the verge of anger. I was already hungry, lonely and tired. HALT. Hungry, angry, lonely, tired. When you get a perfect score, you get a prize. My prize would be a pint of ale. In a frosted glass. Lovely.

I switched my thoughts to something more

rewarding. Like — I was going to get to Greenville early enough to take a dip before dinner. I hadn't been swimming yet this year. The water would still be too cold, too cold for anyone except a madwoman like Nell St. John who went in on Memorial Day regardless. I hoped for a nice bass. It was too hot to pick the bones of a pickerel or perch.

It turned out to be perch. About a dozen of them. Some yellow, some white.

"Couldn't pull them in fast enough," Nell said. "They heard you'd be here for supper I guess."

Nell's house was white frame with a porch and several gables. It sat at the end of a long dirt drive, not more than thirty feet from the shore of Moosehead Lake. It had been in her husband's family for generations. Each summer we scraped and painted a section of it. This summer we were scheduled to do the porch.

Nell's vegetable garden faced southeast and covered nearly a quarter acre including the squash and pumpkin patch whose vines stretched out over the summer lawn. Two giant elms, untouched by disease, still adorned her front yard, and a sugar maple provided shade on summer afternoons, and in spring, sap for maple syrup. Out back a couple of apple trees still produced fruit enough for cider and to dry for winter. Perennials blossomed all summer and fall, from June lilacs through autumn hydrangea. The annuals, like marigolds and cosmos, bloomed continuously from the end of May which was when she planted them from sets she started the last week of February.

She had made bread pudding for desert. She made it like custard. "I'm all ears," she announced over coffee.

"Not much to tell," I said. "Don't you want to work in the garden while it's still light?"

"You wouldn't believe the black flies this year," she said, gesturing toward the kitchen door where the edges of the glass were dark with them. Tiny, no bigger than the head of a pin, they swarmed from the first warm day in May until the Fourth of July.

A little known fact: Black flies don't like beer. The beer has to be taken internally to work.

"They bad this year?"

"I guess. Hey, I want to hear what you been up to. The garden can wait."

Somewhere half way through my narrative I lost her. It was only a little past seven but she got up and started on the dishes. "I'll do those, Nell," I said.

"No. You be company tonight. Besides, I want to hear all you been up to."

I didn't bother to point out that she'd stopped listening. I pulled out my notebook and looked over my report for Claire Du Lac. We left for the meeting a half hour early. "It's just as well we do," Nell assured me. "Sue could use help settin' up."

I'd found early in our relationship that it was no good prodding Nell. Open, babbling like a brook during spring runoff most of the time, if she was questioned she'd freeze right over. Something was bothering her, something, apparently, that I'd said. I tried for a while to pinpoint where in my story she'd gone off. But then I let it go. She'd come around. She always did. Like the brook.

31

I was in bed, ready to turn off my light when she knocked on my door.

"Come on in. What's up?"

Like fruit her trouble had ripened and was ready to fall. "Tell me about Sid," she said.

"Not much to tell. I met him. I thought he was odd."

"Why? How did he seem?"

"Let's see." How to describe that remoteness, the feeling I had that Sid's eyes saw a different landscape, a bleaker one, inside, than the one I saw, or than any I had ever seen. "He seemed detached. Never looked at me."

"Is he well?"

"Yeah. I guess. He's scruffy."

"He's my nephew."

The fruit when it fell, fell apart. I looked at the pieces. "Your nephew. On his mother's side or his father's?" The words were out before I knew they were coming.

"Not funny, Brigid," she said crossly. Then, "You don't know who the father was, do you?"

"No more'n I know who his mother was."

"His mother is my half-sister, Jackie."

Sid's mother is. Sid's father was. It didn't seem possible.

"Not David Thorne!"

She nodded, full of gloom.

I worked on it a while, "Who are you afraid for, Nell?" I asked. "Your sister or Sid?"

"I'm not *afraid*," she declared, "for anyone."

"Well. You know what I mean."

"I just don't want them railroading Sid."

32

"Did he know? That David was his father?"

"No, of course he didn't."

Her eyes shifted from mine, gathered strength from the shadows in the corner of the room before returning, fierce again and determined. "Sid never knew. Really."

"Well then. You don't have anything to worry about," I reassured her, wondering how long Sid had known and whether the resentment he bore his father was strong enough for murder.

"I don't trust Claire Du Lac."

I sorted it out for a while before I answered her. "Do you think I would help her frame Sid?"

"No! Of course not. But that's some smart old lady."

"And I'm not," I said bitterly. Wouldn't consent to frame him, but could be duped into it.

"Look, Brigid." Nell began to stroke my arm. "Let's not fight. I just had an idea."

"Yeah."

"Don't tell the old lady anything about me."

"And tell you everything I tell her," I said, rounding the circle.

When Nell smiled, she looked about eighteen, especially there in the shadow, her hair looking blonde, the network of wrinkles in her cheeks invisible. "Yeah! Why not!" Except for the dry pitch of age, her voice was adolescent with enthusiasm.

"Sounds okay to me," I said grudgingly, as always charmed by her. "H.O.P.E. has the copyright to the history. But far's I know, I hold the copyright to my investigation."

I slept that night as the just are supposed to. I

didn't worry much about the ethics of my promise to Nell until I was sitting across from Claire Du Lac in the gloomy elegance of her Quebec parlor the next day.

Chapter 4

I went on a toot that Saturday night. I do, in a dream, once every three months or so. It always begins with a bunch of us sitting around, shooting the breeze. Nell offers me a drink. Of course I say no. But then she says, "Hey! It's okay. One or two never hurt anyone. You're just not supposed to get drunk." After that I drink myself into oblivion. The first time it happened was a week or two before my first anniversary and it scared the shit out of me. Came to find out the dream was normal. "It's just a warning," Nell reassured me. "We call it a dry drunk.

It means go to more meetings and work your program." The next day I always have a wicked hangover. Just like the one I had Sunday driving back down to Surry.

I spent that Saturday night at the Hotel Terrasse, as close as I'll ever get to spending one in the Chateau Frontenac. I was invited once to spend the weekend there. But it was a package deal and tied with too many strings. An invitation from Heidi, sent with long-stemmed roses. Heidi, the twins' "other mother." Heidi, grimly censorious, or grimly patronizing. Grim, anyhow, in her double-breasted, pin-striped jackets and skirts with the kick-pleat in back. The kick-pleat necessary to accommodate her stride when she toured the Mitchell-Lama building sites designed by her small firm of architects. The twins still go to her for motherly advice. And when they're broke.

Those roses from Heidi, they're the only roses anyone ever sent me. But at the time they seemed funereal, the funeral mine. "Come back," read the note she had tucked among the stems. Once I had returned from detox, she had written, she would take me for a weekend to the Chateau Frontenac in Quebec City. At the time I didn't think my problem was alcohol; my problem, I thought, was Heidi. Ever since she stopped drinking, she'd been a pain in the butt. I kept the roses and threw her invitation away.

The Frontenac embodies for me so many notions of romance, which at fifty-two are probably irreplaceable, that I think I would no longer risk losing them. So I stay down the street at a modest family hotel and keep intact those celluloid images formed when I was young.

My appointment with Claire Du Lac was at four o'clock Saturday afternoon. I felt, as I walked through the park to her house, the first twinge of guilt for my easy agreement to Nell's plan. Not that it seemed unreasonable. I hadn't, after all, intended to tell Du Lac that my landlady, Nell St. John, was half-sister to a woman whom her murdered son-in-law had raped one summer night a quarter century ago. What would have been the point? Why had Nell told me? But to withhold the information, now that I had it, that was different. There was no reason *to* tell, but there was every reason *not not* to tell. I felt sure a logician could plot it on a chart and come up with the correct answer. For me it was a muddle, and by the time I was face-to-face with Claire Du Lac in her gloomy parlor I was at a moral ebb, a moral disadvantage. Even Jesus on the mantel with his bleeding heart seemed disapproving. Just last Tuesday he had seemed to be only slightly bored.

I had been shown into the parlor by the same young woman who answered the door the last time. She was slight and attractive and wore a simple black uniform of some shiny synthetic material. Claire Du Lac addressed her in rapid French of which I caught only a word or two. She appeared a few minutes later with a tea tray.

"My great-niece," Claire offered the information to me with a cup. "Earl Gray. I hope you like it."

I don't. But I took it.

"I think what we do is, you make your report,

then I ask questions. After, we talk about your plans for the week. If I have ideas, then I tell you."

My report was brief enough. I managed not to utter, "I've only had two days," or "It took some time just to settle in."

She didn't seem distressed. Her first question surprised me. "Will you spend the night in Greenville?"

"I hadn't planned to."

She simply nodded. I wondered where I could find a logician to chart my dilemma. She knew about Nell. How much did she know? And how much ought I to tell her?

She passed on to other subjects. "So everyone is helpful. Good. Sometimes Edith is, how do you say, prickly. And you work on the history. That is important. People notice. And it is a good work."

By the way she said good work, I knew she meant the kind that gets you into heaven.

The parlor of her town house overlooked the Parc des Gouverneurs and I could hear faint outdoor sounds of children playing, calling to each other in chirpy voices. The air inside seemed dusty and I could detect the faint odor of incense and sweet smelling wax from an offertory candle. The diamond raindrop trapped on the anemone by my side, in shadow, looked like paste or plastic.

"What are your plans for next week?" she asked.

My plans? Edith had instructed me to do two things: To find out whether Ed knew who Sid's father was, and to find out from Ed why Angele hadn't gone to her husband's memorial Thursday night. Now that I knew the name of Sid's father, it wasn't clear to me how significant it might be

38

whether Ed knew. I alluded to Edith's second order. "I think it's interesting your daughter didn't go to her husband's memorial Thursday night."

"You think it's interesting," replied the mother. "The gossip mills, they must not grind how they used to, or you don't investigate very hard. My daughter's a drunk."

Now there was a subject I knew something about. And I could add as far as two, as in one drunk plus one drunk equals a couple of drunks. Edith's advice, "Ask Ed." I wondered whether he called it an affair. I wondered what he called giving me the run-around. And I wondered whether Claire Du Lac knew what Edith knew about Angele and Ed.

"Your son-in-law seemed well-liked," I offered.

For a while she said nothing. Finally, judiciously, she said, "He was."

Did she know about that long ago rape or didn't she? Should I retrieve my honor with her and risk Nell's confidence, or let it go?

"Did you find out about Genevieve?" she asked, giving it the French pronunciation, zhan-a-vee-ev.

"No." Genevieve. I had not even heard the name.

"I'm surprised Edith said nothing. Or Ed. She is my granddaughter. She's a novice at the convent there in Surry."

Convent? In Surry? That crossroads that seemed to hold nothing but a grocery store and H.O.P.E.? I longed to say, I've only been there two days and it took a while to settle in. But I managed without.

"Try to visit her next week. It's a cloistered order, but while she's a novice, they probably grant permission. Call Sr. Patricia. Tell her I request it."

"Why?" I asked.

"You are the investigator, Miss Donovan. Would you like more tea?"

"No thanks." My stomach grumbled.

"I think it is time you speak with Angele."

"Yes. I planned to do that. I've only been there two days and it took a while to settle in," I said, finally.

She looked at me reprovingly, as I knew she would. "Call me mid-week. We see then if you need to come next weekend."

I walked around the city for an hour, and after dinner I people-watched on the broad terrace by the funicular, overlooking the St. Lawrence. At 9:00 I went in search of the gay bar on Côte Sainte Genevieve, around the corner from Claire Du Lac's, I thought. The woman in the information office had written the address in a round hand that was hard to read. L'Amour Sorcier, it looked like. 789 Côte Sainte Genevieve. Not finding it, I went back to my hotel and my dream toot.

Next day, on my way home, I decided to catch the 8:00 p.m. meeting at St. John's in Bangor. It was one I'd never been to before.

Arriving home after the meeting I reflected that Gram Du Lac had not mentioned Sid. It made me uneasy.

Chapter 5

Monday morning was the sort that drives otherwise sane people to abandon careers, and family even, to move to Maine where the chance of employment, never mind career, is slight, and the lakes they so love to swim in in August, they can drive a truck on from December through March.

I woke with the sun a little before four. Measles, a spotted cat who either came with my cell or had fallen in love with me, slept purring on my chest. A pro-musica medley of birdsong poured in my window.

I pulled sweat pants and shirt over my pajamas, picked up my water pail and, barefoot, went out.

It was nippy. Patches of fog lay here and there on the meadow. In one of these, Beatrice, my pregnant Holstein, stood ruminating, only her head, cheshire cow-like, visible above the mist. A curl of smoke decorated Edith's chimney and I wondered whether she too was up, whether her barometer reading was high today.

My "cell" was one of four tiny cabins, retreat houses for visitors and volunteers, laid out in an arc at the edge of the pasture next to the woods. In the center stood a pump, attached to it, a tin cup on a string. The down stroke, as I pumped my morning water, sounded like a creature in agony.

"You'll wake Edith, you know."

The voice was so surly and unexpected that I screamed and dropped my pail, the icy water splashing over my feet and pants.

"Shush," he said.

Sid was very tall, over six feet, and he was lean and muscular. His eyes were a curiously pale blue, his hair, even his lashes, almost white. His skin, too, was white, but like fresh cream, a tint of yellow in it, and without blemish, without those patches of pigment so often seen in albinos. His eyes reminded me of Nell's. Nell's hair, too, was pale, silvery pale, but her skin was so weathered, so covered with the brown spots of age, that it was impossible to guess what pigment it might have had fifty years or so ago. It could have been creamy. In winter. In summer she was always out in the sun.

Sid picked up my pail. It seemed so small in his

hand. He smelled of the pungent odor of rural poverty, of dung and wood smoke, of earth and sweat. He began furiously to pump water. After two or three strokes the handle stopped complaining.

"I thought you were afraid to wake Edith," I aspirated, a whispered shout. I was angry, and shaken.

For the first time he looked at me, a glance only, but potent with rage. He snorted and handed me the pail, brimming over, too heavy. His eyes fastened now on some distant semaphore. "Who could sleep through your yelling?" he muttered. "She's up now. Fire's started."

He was looking at the smoke placidly spiraling skyward from Edith's chimney.

"Asshole!" I exploded. "That chimney was smoking when I got up."

But I was talking to myself. Sid, uncannily, had disappeared. Only his odor lingered. Feeling bullied and aggrieved I returned to my cell, heated some water, washed and had a cup of tea. I wondered where Sid lived and made an entry in the back of my notebook at the end of a growing list of things I needed to find out.

And then I tried to center myself, concentrating on those facts I had already managed to uncover. Randomly they seemed to surface. Claire Du Lac's son-in-law, David Thorne, had raped a young woman who, it turned out, was my landlady Nell's younger sister. Sid, the surly young man at the pump just now, was the product of that long ago act of violence. David Thorne's wife, Angele, was a drunk. And she and my buddy Ed Kelly were probably lovers. I noted, dispassionately, my heart react. Mildly curious, I wondered why. Jealousy of Ed was out of the question.

Not much to go on. But it was early days. Claire Du Lac wanted me to look up her daughter, Angele, and the granddaughter, Genevieve. I hadn't been in a convent since the day I'd left my own. I did the arithmetic in my head. Fifty-seven from eighty-nine. It would be thirty-two years come August first. A few twenty-four hours ago.

For the next two hours, until seven, I devoted myself to the history of H.O.P.E. By the time my stomach started to growl, I had finished mapping it out. I put the annotated outline of chapters in an envelope. On the outside I wrote *Edith Wardwell* and on my way to the parking lot, I stuck it under her door. I couldn't tell whether grey smoke still rose from her chimney. The blazing sun had bleached away color as it had burned off the early morning fog. Some young volunteers at the water pump were shouting and having a water fight, so I was sure she was awake.

I stopped in Ellsworth for breakfast, at Dick's on Main Street, at the light right after the little bridge across the Union River on the edge of town. I always stop there on my way to Mount Desert, even if it's just for coffee and a piece of pie. Only locals go there. Locals and me. It must be masochism on my part, because they sure don't make me feel I belong. And there are no breakfast specials to attract the tourist trade. Still I prefer it to McDonald's. I ordered two dropped eggs, dark toast and coffee. The coffee is weak but the cup has no bottom.

The tide, I saw crossing the causeway to Mount

Desert Island, or MDI as they call it, was high, the water deep blue, nearly black, and the sky, like porcelain, seemed almost to shine, such a Della Robbia blue it was by contrast. Here and there dark and northern, islands of pointed fir, like cut-outs, rose stark against the translucent sky. The rich, unseen under their sails, cavorted across the bays, East and West, on either side. Cadillac Mountain and three other egg-like domes of granite that dominate the island from afar were no longer visible, having dropped from sight behind the fringe of woods at the island's edge. I took the right fork, following the sign to Swan's Island Ferry. Angele lived on the Somes Sound side of North East Harbor.

The Thorne cottage was a disappointment. I'd expected one of those sprawling edifices New York and Philadelphia wealth had spawned on the islands off Maine's coast at the turn of the century and in the twenties before the crash. Thorne's wasn't modest, just modern, tiered and terraced, boarded and battened, and crenelated with a half dozen solar panels. It was most likely equipped with windy clivus multrums, those composting toilets introduced into Maine by Abby Rockefeller. I was glad I'd used the restroom when I stopped at the Texaco to ask directions. I had decided to risk not calling first. But she seemed to be expecting me.

Angele's age was hard to tell, she was in those middle years, her hair expertly blonde and soft, her skin smooth — but preserved, not fresh — torso firm, red eyes obscured by lenses lightly tinted; obscured also by the outsized frames of her glasses was the giveaway flesh below her eyes. A liberty silk scarf concealed her throat; below it, on a tapered swell of

her breasts, youthfully sweatered in a silky knit, lay
a golden tangle of chains. Everything about her was a
pale shade of gold. She looked rich, like cream. Not
New York, not Philadelphia, but still a lot of class, a
lot of glamour. I wondered how much Ed was still
able to notice. We sat and had tea beside a wall of
glass overlooking the sound and, in the distance, the
islands stepping out toward Spain.

I had apologized for disturbing her and been
reassured. My commiserations over her husband's
death had been graciously received. My tea, I assured
her, was perfect. It was Earl Gray.

"How can I help you?" she said.

If her mother hadn't told me she was a drunk, I
would have missed it, attributed to nerves and sorrow
the stiff detachment of her manner, her schizoid way
of talking, as if she were reciting lines, recognizing
them as not well-written, not really worth the effort.

I fed her my line about the history, about wanting
to interview people connected with H.O.P.E.

"But why me?" she asked listlessly.

There was only one truthful answer I could give
and my imagination had not, on the long ride there,
come up with a plausible alternative. "Your mother
suggested I call on you."

"Mother?"

"Yes. I saw her Saturday." I had introduced
myself on the strength of that information, but it
seemed she was hearing it now for the first time. I
wondered whether she was operating in a blackout.
She retrieved her fumble. She'd had lots of practice.

"Of course. Well, how can I help?"

"Do you mind if I tape this?"

A look of alarm seeped across her face marring

46

the bland serenity. She pressed a tissue to her lips as if to blot out the emotion. "Must you?"

"Well, I'd really be grateful. I don't take shorthand. And if I take notes, it's hard to follow the conversation."

She knew about having difficulty following conversations. She pointed at a seashell on the wall beside her chair, a few inches above the thick white carpet. "The outlet," she explained. The shell pulled out and, behind it, as she said, lay the nasty practicality of an outlet.

To put her at ease, I chattered while I elaborated my preparations, opening my notebook, setting out a couple of pens.

"Do you know Alex Katz?" I asked.

On an inner wall hung a huge portrait of his wife, Ada, sipping from a glass beaded with condensation, oddly cropped tiger lilies and heads of children on either side of her, her own face cropped at the bridge of the giant sunglasses she wore, so that the iced tea rather than Ada seemed to be the focus of the picture. "I never saw that one before," I said.

"Oh yes," she agreed.

To what, seemed unimportant. I thought she was pleased that I had noticed. "You the collector?"

She nodded.

Facing Ada were two Neil Wulliver's, one of summer trees, another a Lincolnville scene in mud season. I laughed. "That's a challenge. Mud season is beautiful." For a moment she came to life and we shared the secret humor of it as if I were the only person, besides herself, who had ever gotten it. Just the two of us and, presumably, Wulliver himself.

47

"Do you know Yvonne?" she asked.

"Jacquette?"

She nodded.

"Yes. Not well."

She inclined her head, a gesture, economic, of inquiry.

"Yeah. I like her stuff a lot. I'm not crazy about the mural in the Federal Building."

She brushed the Federal Building mural aside. She rose and beckoned me, the index finger of her right hand crooked. The nail, a pale lavender, had been broken and repaired.

At the end of a long, pale blue hall, pale blue carpet, pale blue walls, hung here and there with weaving, Native American sweet grass and anywhere-modern, was her bedroom, cream again and pale yellow. On the wall behind the bed was an acre of painting, vivid oils, an aerial scene, not of Maine, but of New York, at night, lights everywhere against a velvet black, tail lights, headlights, rivers of light, some red, some white, and the fragile arcs of light holding up the fairy nighttime weight of the George Washington bridge. I had only seen photos of it before.

My silence was the compliment she seemed most to want. After a while, by some unspoken mutual consent, we returned to the glass wall overlooking the sound and our interview.

I handed her the mike and showed her the red switch. "You can control what's recorded. Here. Just turn it on and off." I was pretty sure that by the time I sat down and picked up my notebook she would forget. It didn't matter. I wouldn't use any of

48

it anyway. It was more for show than anything. I leaned over to check that the recorder was running.

"Have you ever visited H.O.P.E.?"

"Oh yes. Many times."

"Would you say a few words about the work they do there?"

She did. But they were very few.

"Would you talk a little about some of the people there?"

She looked blank. I decided to risk it.

"I met an odd young man there," I confided. She seemed to be becoming bored. "I don't know his last name. Maybe he hasn't one. Sid."

The change in her was remarkable. Her face seemed to melt, to grow soft like butter on a summer day. The mike fell, unnoticed, from her hand.

"You okay?"

"Excuse me." She raised herself from her chair.

She seemed suddenly elderly, made-up, a caricature of what she would someday probably become. She crossed the room silently, her body slight, weightless on the deep pile of the carpet. She seemed so alone, a body lost in a mausoleum, everything about her drained of life, of color, the only life left mere representations of it in the pictures on the walls, like offerings in Egyptian tombs to accompany the dead and the soon-to-be-dead on their journeys. Without a collision she navigated the islands of furniture. I heard water running and then her voice briefly. She must have called someone. I wondered if it was Ed. When she returned her color was high again and I could detect the faint network of red in her cheeks, cheeks which would never require the tint of rouge for color. In addition to the odor of her perfume, I now detected about her the agreeable smell of mint, from mouthwash or some other "breathsaver."

"I woke," she said, "with a headache. Sinus."

"I'm sorry."

She patted the air with her fingertips. "It's nothing. I'm used to it. But I really don't think I can go on with this interview."

My co-alcoholic needs surged up in me, cavalry to the rescue, trumpets sounding. I love you, I love your paintings, I love everything in you that's struggling to stay alive. Let me take you away and make it all well. The meeting tonight in Ellsworth is supposed to be terrific. There's one in Bar Harbor too. And, of course, if you're really not ready yet, we could have a drink and talk about it.

"Sure," is what I actually said, fumbling with the equipment, wondering whether, if I took the time to put it properly in its case, I would refuse the drink she was on the verge of offering me.

God grant me the serenity . . . I groped. Serenity to accept a pleasant afternoon and evening talk with my old friend Ed and my new one Angele. What could be so wrong in that?

"I know it's early," she began.

"Yes, it is. Hey, I'm sorry about barging in on you like this. And I'm really grateful to you." I slung the mike on its cord over my shoulder, scooped my notebook and pens into my jacket pocket, tucked the recorder under my arm and held out my hand. The palm of hers was damp, but she shook mine with a firm grip. She looked into my eyes and for a moment I could see through all the protective lenses into that dizzy void of another's soul. I teetered on the edge of

50

it, tempted, oh so tempted by those dark, inviting waters. At the bottom the pot of gold, the brass ring. But there was no bottom, or none that I could reach. What I had not yet been able to convince myself of is that there is never a pot of gold, never a brass ring, never even anything to rescue. In Angele the massacre had taken place a long, long time ago. And, in her mind at least, the perpetrator's name was Sid. Why, I couldn't imagine.

Driving off the island I managed, one hand on the wheel, to check my meeting book. The closest noon meeting was in Bangor. I'd never make it. I thought Edith could keep me out of mischief for the afternoon. If she was willing to.

Chapter 6

The sound of laughter surprised me as I approached Edith's door.

It was Sid laughing, sitting at the trestle table, a cup of coffee in his hand. Seeing me, he scowled, and scowling looked more like himself.

"Come on in," Edith invited. "Wanna cuppa?"

"Oh no. Just poking my head in to say hello. Catch ya' later."

"Brigid, come in. I want you and Sid to get to know each other. If you don't want coffee I still have some of that apple juice."

"Coffee sounds great."

"Cups are on the counter. To your right . . ."

"Facing the sink." The three of us said it together. Sid laughed again. I liked the sound.

The coffee dispenser, a large thermos with a spout, sat on the table in front of Sid. He took my cup and filled it, a cigarette clamped between his teeth, the curling smoke getting into his eyes, watering them. He thrust the cup at me, angry again.

"What do you take in it?" asked Edith.

"Nothing. Just black." I was unreasonably disappointed that she hadn't remembered.

"Of course," she said. "I remember." And I felt mollified. "You're a member of the club. I told Sid when a squeaking pump, especially *that* squeaking pump'd wake Edith in the morning, that's saying she was still asleep in the morning, that'd be the day."

Neither Sid nor I said anything, Sid too busy examining how the tobacco burned at the tip of his cigarette, me looking for clues to my future in the depths of my cup.

"What've you been up to today, Brigid?" Edith asked.

"Went down to MDI."

"Oh?"

"Gram wanted me to see Angele."

Sid turned and, for the second time, looked directly at me, the pale blue of his eyes turned grey, like ash that hides the burning of a coal. "Angele who? I hate that woman," he muttered and started to rise, roughly knocking aside Edith's restraining hand.

"Sid! Sit down!" Her voice, peremptory, like the crack of a lion tamer's whip, worked. Growling, Sid sat down again.

53

Edith said, "Well, we've had a busy morning too. Sid finished mowing the lawn here. I laid the woof for some table mats. And the good nuns up to the cloisters called and asked if I knew someone willing to mow their field. I said I thought I did. Sid and I were just talking it over. He needs a ride up there."

I recognized in her eyes the invitation to help. I said, "Oh yeah?"

"Yeah," replied Edith, "and I think you are the answer to our prayer. Would you mind running him up?"

Would you mind dreadfully getting into that little cage with this nice tame lion? "No problem," I said.

"Okay, Sid? Now you behave yourself."

Behave himself. Big deal.

Sid, growling and mumbling inaudibly, pushed himself back from the table and headed out the door. I rose more slowly, more reluctantly, turned to say, of all things, thank you. Edith winked at me and whispered, "He likes older women better. He's afraid the younger ones are after his body."

"Say what! Then why doesn't he like me?"

"I guess he finds you young and beautiful."

"And when were you last in Ireland?"

"What are you doing for dinner tonight?"

I hadn't thought. The first two nights I'd eaten supper at a diner on Route 176.

"I have two Budget Gourmet dinners."

"Sure, that'd be nice."

Sid maintained a grumpy silence the whole way. Following Edith's instructions, I punched the trip mileage button as I turned onto 176. At three point four miles, just as she said, a rutted track turned off into the woods. I hoped I wouldn't lose my oil pan.

The convent turned out to be a long two-story building with a gambrel roof. It looked, like so many Maine houses, as if it had grown in fits and starts, in response to need with never enough money. One section was finished with cedar shingles, silvering nicely with age, but much was tar paper crazy-quilted with strips of lathing. Roll roofing, black for the most part, but with patches of dark green, covered the roof. Two dormers, like afterthoughts, jutted from the gambrel slope. The dooryard was a mess, packed dirt, rocks and clutter, except for one small flower bed of marigolds serving as a shrine to some mendicant saint, Anthony or Francis, his arms outstretched in a diminutive blessing. Further back stood a small gabled barn surrounded by a meadow, the one, apparently, that Sid was to mow. Suddenly a black garbed figure, her back turned toward us, her arms waving above her head, burst from the barn shouting. A pig, big and fast, ran her down and headed in our direction.

"Sugar!" exclaimed the nun on the ground. Another nun appeared in the doorway. "Stop that pig!"

Stop *that* pig? Oh yeah?

"Get out," Sid yelled, "and wave your arms." He jumped out his side and started yelling and carrying on. The pig took a quick look at him and veered toward my side of the car.

"Stop that pig!" the nuns, black and furious, stood and shouted. "You! Stop that pig!"

Me. Me! And then, there I was, somehow, out of the car, the pig no more than twenty feet away and bearing down like a tractor trailer out of control, closing the distance fast.

"Yell!" shouted Sid.

So I started hollering and carrying on, scared shitless, eyes closed.

"You can shut up now," Sid growled. I opened my eyes. Lying close by my feet, panting and laughing, was the pig.

"Where'd you learn to holler like that?" the second nun asked me. She and Sid secured a rope around the pig's belly.

"You think that's going to hold her?" I asked, incredulous.

"Oh, Charley just needs her exercise," she said. "The rope's a formality. She'll go back now for her dinner. Sid, will you help Genevieve?" She too gave it the French pronunciation.

Genevieve, her habit soiled, and Sid trotted Charley back to the barn.

"I'm Sister Pat," the woman said, thrusting out her hand.

I took it firmly in my own. She smelled, but faintly, like Sid. So did my hand when she relinquished it.

"I'm Brigid Donovan."

"I know. We've been expecting you. And thanks for bringing Sid to us, too." She laughed as with pleasure at some flash of insight. She said, "God has kept you busy this morning. Would you like some refreshment? Our mint is up and we brewed a pitcher of mint tea. Our first of the season." She had pulled off her coif revealing thick, wavy hair of stunning coppery red, so surprisingly thick and abundant, so

56

surprisingly red for a woman whose age I'd taken to be forty-five or so.

"Henna!"

"Henna?"

"My hair. It kept me out of the convent ten years at least. Then I decided if I really did have a vocation — and I thought I really did — I shouldn't let my hair stop me. I mean, some nuns chew bubble gum! I know some redheads — on the outside —" She leaned toward me to share this confidence, "who pluck the grey ones." She drew back and sighed. "Doesn't help really. The red fades. It's not just the grey."

She was oddly beautiful, a Modigliani lopsidedness to her Celtic features. A garden of coppery hairs sprouted from a mole on her cheek, near the bold line of her jaw. Her teeth, when she laughed, and she often did, broke eagerly from her mouth, jostling each other, it seemed, to be first. Her eyes, diamond-shaped under finely arched dark brows, glinted blue in the sun like clear ice.

My stomach growled, a long, audible rumble.

"Perfect!" exclaimed Sr. Pat. "God's not done with you today. She must want you to test our cheese. Come along!"

She linked her arm through mine and drew me toward the house. "This is the Cloisters," she said with a flourish, a broad inclusive gesture of her arm.

Oh yeah? "Cloisters?" I said.

"Well. It's a little premature to *call* it the Cloisters. But along here —" Her hand swept the front of the house, "and then straight back to the barn. That's where they'll be. So we can do our chores and not get wet. Our kitchen garden, herbs and stuff, they'll all be there, in back, inside the cloisters."

I could tell that for this strangely intense woman the cloisters conceived were cloisters present. That as she walked in the imaginary courtyard, doing chores, she could hear the silver notes of some heavenly harp. It was probably just as well, I reflected, that she had allowed herself the vanity of that very real crop of well-tended red hair.

The front door opened into a large room carpeted with a variety of old rugs including at the entrance a worn, machine-made oriental with a large Rorschach stain in the upper quadrant. Opposite the door along the far wall stood a slate sink and hand pump, open cupboards with dishes, pots and pans, and canned goods, and a large old-fashioned iron cookstove. To the left stood a long picnic table and benches. To the right, a collection of ancient furniture: sofas, armchairs, rockers, footstools.

On a shelf by the front window, St. Joseph, a wooden rosary draped around his neck and baby Jesus in his arms, seemed to preside over the living area. The entire wall beside them was lined with books.

"Sit down," she said. "Or maybe you want to wash your hands. Over there. Use a paper towel."

It was awkward pumping and rinsing at the same time. She cut several thick slices from a loaf of dark bread and put them on the table. There were two plates of cheese, both soft.

"From Adele," she said. "The goat. This one's plain and this has herbs in it. We thought if we could get it right we could sell it. What do you think?"

The herb one was very good. I wasn't so sure about the other. "Well, if you've got any of the herb cheese for sale, I'd love to buy some. How much are you asking for it?"

"I don't know. Ten dollars a pound?"

I choked a while.

"I agree. That's what Barney suggested. Sister Barnabas. I think it's too much too. But you must take some. For your help. Don't tell Barney, though," she added conspiratorially.

After a while I asked how many of them there were.

"Right now just the three of us, Barney, Genevieve and I. I guess you want to talk with Gen."

Surprised, I looked at her inquiringly.

"The old lady called. I shouldn't call her that. Mrs. Du Lac. Last night. Afraid we wouldn't let Gen talk with you. She seems not to have heard of Vatican Two."

Sr. Pat began to laugh again. I liked the sound of it. I liked the way her teeth popped out when she took her hand away from her mouth. She seemed to have a hard time stopping. At last she wiped her eyes and said, "I got to thinking of the look on Mrs. Du Lac's face when she first saw poor Genevieve's convent. I know she imagined it all marble and gold candlesticks."

Whereas, I understood, it's really green lawns and peacefully cloistered herb gardens. "What do you do with the pig?" I asked.

"Besides chase her? Barney again. Says we can

59

sell pigs to pay our taxes. We never have. We keep the piglets until they're pets and then give them away to people who solemnly swear never to butcher them. If you think kittens are hard to get rid of . . ."

The door opened and Genevieve appeared, a bucket of milk in her hand.

"This is Brigid, that your grandmother called about. I've sold her a pound of your herb cheese. She loves it. Thinks ten dollars is a bit steep. But we've agreed on a price."

Genevieve looked mortified. "Oh, you mustn't pay us. Please. It was so good of you to stop Charley."

It seemed clear these women would have a struggle paying their taxes. I wondered whether they would accept a ten dollar donation. It turned out they would. However, they didn't call it a donation from me, they called it a gift from God. "Oh! Look what God has given us today!" Genevieve said, clapping her hands. "Thank you, God." Pat nudged me and whispered, "And thank you too, Brigid. God certainly has kept you busy doing Her work this morning!"

After lunch, Pat left Genevieve and me to talk alone. "Call me, Gen, if you need me," she said. "it's been a hard week for Gen," she reminded me — perhaps she was warning me, leaving to me the responsibility not to probe too deeply with my questions.

But I had no idea then what pain lay beneath the sweet covering of innocence and youth that was Genevieve Thorne, no idea what questions I was being told not to ask. I've often wondered had I

known any part of Gen's story and had interviewed
her differently whether it all might have turned out
some other way.

Chapter 7

I saw in Genevieve a woman purified, as if the primordial life force, filtered through three generations of women, had left in her, the last, very little of the grit that characterized her grandmother, and none of the poison that had corrupted her mother. I offered my condolences for her father's death.

"He was a good man, a saint," she replied, her voice soft but urgent. "I'm only grateful God let him stay with us this long."

"Had he been ill?" I asked, surprised. No one had mentioned anything of the sort.

"Ill? No. Why do you ask? Oh no, I just meant . . . You know. We say, 'God isn't finished with us yet.' Meaning He is giving us time to work on our faults. I think He let Dad stay here with us as long as He did just to help us. I only meant that Dad . . . Well, I know no one is perfect — except Jesus, of course. Not even saints. But . . . Pat warns me all the time against the sin of idolatry, and I know I must watch out. But I can't help it, can I?" She looked at me imploringly, her eyes large, chocolate brown under the firm line of her brows. "I know he wasn't perfect. It's just that I truly don't know of anything he ever did wrong."

Well, investigative genius that I am, I could tell her one thing her father had done that was wrong, very wrong. I thought of Genevieve and her half brother, Sid, working together earlier. The contrast between them was bizarre. Genevieve purified, and Sid murky with the sediment of generations, thrust into being by an act of violence committed a quarter century ago.

"My brother and I have talked about it," she said. Her tone slightly belligerent, a challenge, it seemed, to me. She knew? They both knew? And still she thought her father a saint? My mind could not conjure an image of Genevieve and Sid discussing the matter. "He agrees with me. Funny isn't it. I mean, so often sons don't like their fathers. For no reason. They just need to. So they can break away, I guess, and grow up. But it was never like that with Paul."

"Who's Paul?"

"My brother. Didn't you know I had a brother?"

As a matter of fact, yes, I did. I didn't know she had two brothers. I let it pass.

"No. Tell me about him."

Her face flushed with enthusiasm. "We're like twins really. Except we don't look anything alike." She looked quickly over her shoulder, a gesture that seemed involuntary, as if to check that no one was listening. "He's dark. I mean really dark. It's so funny. He's working — as a volunteer, not for pay — at the Emmaus Hotel in Harlem. Have you ever heard of it? Well, it's really a shelter more than a hotel and it's run by a priest. Anyway Paul wrote and said he passes there." She burst into laughter, innocent and infectious and I laughed with her. "He passes! In Harlem!"

As so often happens, when the shower of laughter passed, our mood had changed and a kind of gloom settled on us. She broke the silence.

"Gram told me you were coming, but she didn't tell me why you wanted to see me."

Problem: she hadn't told me either.

"Well, you see," I tried, "I'm writing a history of H.O.P.E. Your grandmother hired me to do that."

"Oh. That's very interesting." She was guileless as a child.

"Yes. Well, I'm interviewing people." She looked puzzled. Well, she might. "Umh. Have you ever worked there, uh, done any volunteer stuff or anything?"

"Oh no."

"Oh. I thought maybe you had."

"No."

"I see."

64

I longed for her innocence, to be able to say to her, "Hey, I'm not sure why your grandmother sent me, except she must believe you've got some information about your father's murder, information that might help to solve the crime." What I said was, "Your grandmother is concerned about you."

"Gram loves me."

The earth is round. God made us to love and obey Him. Gram loves me. The simplicity of her mind was like a catechism. "Yes, she does. She certainly does. And she loved your father."

"That's a lie."

There was no heat in it. Just a correction: Setting things straight. Gram did not love David Thorne. I was mistaken.

"Oh. Well, she does want to find out who murdered him."

At the word, she sucked her breath in sharply, as if she had been struck. "We all do. Poor man. He desperately needs our help."

I was taken aback by her reply, but I had to agree. "Yes. He probably does."

"If Sr. Pat or I can help. He could stay here. I've thought about it. We could pray together. At first, when I first heard, I wanted him punished. I wanted revenge. I wanted to hurt him." Her eyes, wide and staring, were witnessing again her crime of vengeance. "But I prayed to St. Joseph." She inclined her head toward the benign figure with the infant in his arms. "Because he's a father, too, you see. And St. Joseph heard my prayer and intervened because the next day I could see how if the man came here and we prayed together, I could be an instrument of God's peace. That maybe God took Father that way for the poor

65

man's salvation." Then, as if offering conclusive proof of God's intentions, she added, "I told Sr. Pat and she agreed. So, if you do find him, he really can come here."

"Well, I'll keep that in mind."

She looked contentedly at her folded hands, anticipating the peace to come, the peace she herself seemed already to enjoy. A peace my next words shattered.

"I spoke with your mother this morning."

Her hands flew apart. She pressed them to her head, her fingers bunching the black material of her veil, stuffing it into the unseen orifices of her ears. "Don't talk to me about her. Don't talk to me about her. Don't talk to me about her. Don't talk to me about her."

When I raised my hand, a gesture only, a signal, conventional in the extreme, for her to stop, she began to scream.

It seemed to me then and ever afterwards that Pat rose from the floor, from Genevieve's feet and simply enveloped her, removed her for a moment from sight, hid her in a black cloud above which hovered a radiant sun of uncoifed hair. Pat rocked her and crooned to her a lullaby, tenderly in French. In a while Gen was calm again. Pat insisted she go lie down. I might as well not have been there.

But when the door closed behind Genevieve, Sr. Pat turned on me angrily. "Have you no decency!"

I was too nonplussed to answer. I had no idea what had shattered Genevieve's sublime composure, nor how Pat had appeared almost instantly at her feet when she began to scream. And I had no idea why Pat was angry with me. I felt innocent and was beginning to feel abused.

"Would you please leave! Now!"

Not many twenty-four hours ago I would have instantly complied, suggesting as I went that Sr. Pat might want to go somewhere and make love with herself. I struggled for a moment to quell that desire. "I don't know what happened," I said. "I've never met anyone who seemed so totally at peace. Then suddenly she started to scream."

"Nonsense! Get out! And tell that evil old woman when you see her that she had better never, ever try this on again. If she ever sends someone to upset that poor child . . . Have you no decency! Has she no pity!"

"I remember what I said," I interrupted. "I said, 'I saw your mother this morning.' That's what I said and then she started yelling. 'Don't talk about her.' She kept repeating it. 'Don't talk about her. Don't talk about her.' "

"I know. That's when I came in to stop you."

"Then she started screaming when she saw you!"

"You raised your hand to strike her. That's why she screamed."

"I did not!" Scratch a nun and find a bully. Some things never change. "Go fuck yourself."

The bench, when I jumped up, fell over with a crash. The noise affected us differently, antagonizing me even more, apparently acting to mollify Pat. I knocked aside the hand she held out to me. "God forgive me," she said.

I think I snarled. Later, Pat said my lip curled just like a dog's.

67

"Please," she said. "I was very upset. I thought perhaps Mrs. Du Lac had sent you to try to take Genevieve away. I'm sorry. Please sit down. And tell me: Why did you come? Why did she send you?"

How should I know why she sent me? Like a pin, the absurdity of my situation pricked the balloon of my anger. I hid my face by picking up the bench. I took my time sitting back down. I looked at Sr. Pat sitting calm and self-assured across from me, the black authority of her robe intimidating.

"I don't know."

"What?"

"I don't know why she sent me."

"But surely . . ." Her incredulity was that of someone who knows, always, what she does and why she does it, the incredulity, in fact, of a bully. Poor Genevieve if Sr. Pat and Claire Du Lac were fighting over her. They wouldn't stop until there was nothing left. There didn't seem to be a whole lot left now except a pool of terror and a pale sheet of calm.

I decided then to level with Sr. Pat. In the words of my favorite country western song, I decided they could take this job and shove it. I needed a week at Chesuncook a lot more than I needed money in the bank.

"Look, an old friend of mine told me a Claire Du Lac wanted someone to write a history of H.O.P.E. And then she asks me to investigate her son-in-law's murder. I took the job. Don't ask me why. But I've just quit. And I'd like to go now and call in my resignation."

She started to laugh. My insides still felt like curdled milk. "What's so funny?"

"Nothing. Everything. Can we start again?"

Something in me did want to know what it was all about. So I stayed. Not for Gram Du Lac. I had no intention of continuing to meddle for her in other people's pain. But for myself. To satisfy my curiosity. I wasn't thinking straight: Everyone knows what curiosity does to cats.

"Yeah?"

"Please. Would you like another glass of tea."

"Sure."

"For some reason I believe you," she said, handing me my glass refilled. It was an invitation as much as a statement of fact. An invitation to spill my guts. I didn't say a word and I sipped my tea. No way was I going to rescue this lady. Listen to her, okay. To whatever she chose to divulge. Then I was heading out to Greenville for the summer.

"I should have known she would use someone like you."

Like me? Clever, etc., you mean? She saw she had skated out on thin ice.

"Discreet."

I nodded.

"Trusting."

And dumb. Real dumb. "Look. It's all right. If you have something to tell me, tell me. I really need to hit the road."

"I wish you wouldn't. Drop the investigation for Mrs. Du Lac, I mean."

"Better the evil known."

"Well, yes, actually. Look, Gen's grandmother has been trying to get her removed from here from the beginning."

"*Get* her removed?"

"Yes. Exactly. Against Gen's will."

"How? Why?"

"How? She came in her bloody big Lincoln Continental with her chauffeur once. Tried to pull Gen out the door. Barney stopped her. Sr. Barnabas."

I could see the scene in my mind. It was grotesque. "But why?"

Pat started to reply then hesitated. Finally she said, without much conviction, "Perhaps she thinks that Gen's is not a true vocation."

I worked it over. I thought taking Gen away might not be such a bad idea. It wouldn't surprise me if the help Genevieve needed was professional and psychiatric. I didn't say anything, just waited. It worked.

"She thinks I'm a bad influence on Gen." Pat appraised my reaction. It wasn't much.

"Oh yeah?"

"You make it difficult."

I make it difficult! Give me a break, sister. I still said nothing.

"I have no right to ask that what I tell you be held in confidence."

It ended on that slightly higher note. The silent air waited for my reassurance: Trust me, Sister, trust me. But we waited quietly, the air and me.

"Angele Thorne and I," she resumed finally, "were at school together. We were inseparable. When we were ten and twelve we became blood sisters. And then, so we could always be together, we decided that when we grew up, we would be nuns. Her mother,

Gram, never approved of me. Never approved of our friendship." As an afterthought, as if to secure my confidence in her, she added, "I don't know why."

I thought I caught in her eyes the memory of why. It seemed, after all these years, still to cause her pain.

I remembered my blood sister. We too were ten. As we approached puberty, my love had deepened. She became "boy crazy." It still hurt, not much but some. There was more than disappointed love bothering Sr. Pat, however. I wondered what else had happened between her and Angele and Mrs. Du Lac.

"That same unreasoning distrust of me —" Pat's voice had risen slightly, revealing her agitation, "seems to have carried over now to Genevieve."

The distrust, yes. And also the cause? I wondered. I recalled the tenderness of Pat's comforting embrace. The thought repelled me. Only a monster, I thought, could take advantage of Gen's pathetic vulnerability. Pat might be a bully, but she didn't seem to be a monster.

"Maybe she just thinks Genevieve needs professional help."

"Maybe." Clearly, there was more to tell. But the good nun with the coppery hair had decided she had revealed enough already. It was time for me to hit the road for Greenville.

"Well, thank you for the tea and cheese."

"Oh. Thank you for stopping Charley," she said politely. Then, urgently, "Brigid! Please. Will you stay on the case?"

I exploded. "Look! I feel like a flying asshole.

You're not the first person's pointed out to me I'm not investigating a murder, what I'm doing's running errands for Claire Du Lac. My good friend Nell thinks Du Lac's setting me up to frame Sid. You think I'm being set up to get Genevieve committed to the funny farm."

"Poor Brigid," she said and the heat of my anger abruptly died. Tears stung my eyes and I braced my hand across my brow, pressing hard, and stared down at the table, it seemed like forever.

In that quiet time I felt myself pulled into the vortex of my past. Whatever it was Pat might ask me to do, I was pretty sure that I would: For her vision of green lawns where I saw only rock and clutter, because she too loved Angele, and for her icy blue eyes and hennaed hair, and because of the inexorable black authority of her habit. She reminded me of my first love, Sr. Anne.

Counting Edith, this made the third time this week and the second time today I had fallen in love.

I should explain: I haven't always fallen in love so easily. Not back when I had a honey, when I made love, or at least had someone to hold at night. But it's been a while since they took Alicia away. And AA meetings aren't as easy as bars for picking someone up. For me they aren't. Not that I'd ever done much of that. Just for a while after I left Heidi. I met Rosemary in a bar. Met her there and lost her there. After that I quit the bar scene. Alicia was a friend of a friend. She, too, preferred to booze at home. When they took her away, they dressed her in a white jacket with these funny arms that tie in back. The only way to keep her from tearing the skin in strips from her arms. She thought she was killing spiders, the ones crawling all over her.

Still, it seemed odd, falling in love with Angele in the morning and, over goat cheese, with Pat in the afternoon. I thought I better be getting on home to Greenville before I landed in some mischief.

Chapter 8

"Well, did she wrap you around her little finger?" asked Edith, first thing when I walked in the door late that afternoon.

I think I blushed, my cheeks felt suddenly warm. "Oh, I don't know," I hedged.

"Oh, oh. I guess she must have. Well, join the party. She's an awfully sweet girl, isn't she?"

Sweet girl? I'd thought she meant Pat. Shifting gears, I said, "Yeah, she's sweet enough. But she's weird."

"Weird? What makes you say that?"

I told her all about it. From stopping Charley to Gen's fit of screaming and Pat's rage.

"I'm surprised," Edith said, "that you're still in one piece." Then she said, "Ed's left messages for you everywhere. Call him after supper. Speaking of which. Do you know how to work a microwave? I'm getting hungry."

Over supper I tested my new information on Edith. "I think I know who Sid's father is."

"Do you."

"Yeah. David Thorne."

"Well, you've gotten around some. Would you pass the salt."

The salt was as close to her as it was to me. I passed it and waited.

"Did Ed tell you that?"

She asked it casually, buttering her bread. It made me think she knew all about David Thorne. What she wasn't sure about was whether Ed had known, and she probably still wanted me to find that out. Find it out for *her*. I felt a surge of annoyance. "I resigned, incidentally."

After a bit of self-conscious chewing, Edith asked, "You're not going to write the history of H.O.P.E.?"

"Not that either."

"Why is that?"

She hadn't batted an eye over my "either." So she knew. Knew I was investigating David Thorne's murder. I wondered how. Because someone, Ed perhaps, had told her? Or had she simply realized it in that psychic way she had?

Suddenly I lost it. "Why? *Why?* Because I'm sick and tired of being everybody's errand girl. Everyone has an agenda for me. Including you!" I accused.

75

She smiled. It made me even angrier. " 'Find out how much Ed knows,' " I mimicked. "And what do I get in return? Zip! I know, by the way, why Angele wasn't at her husband's memorial Thursday night. But would you tell me? Oh, no. Gram Du Lac gets the honor of doing that. 'Some kind of investigator you are,' she says. 'Don't know my daughter Angele's the town drunk.' The two of them, right? Ed and Angele. They're drinking buddies. You could've told me."

Edith said, "There's ice cream for dessert."

While I cleared the table and spooned out the ice cream, I cooled down some.

She said, "So, you're giving up because I didn't — I'd just met you now — and I didn't tell you everything, every piece of gossip, all the rumors. You know what I think?"

"No, but I'm sure you're going to tell me."

"I think you bit off more than you can chew. I think you're finding it's a lot harder than researching a murder that happened fifty years ago."

I looked at her, surprised. She picked up the book lying open, face down without a dust jacket, by her side. "Yours," she said. "It's good."

"Thanks."

It doesn't take much manipulation to get me jumping through hoops, barking for more. But this time I wasn't having any. "Maybe you're right," I said. "Maybe it is more than I can handle."

We ate our ice cream a while in silence. Edith said, "You don't have to follow anyone's agenda, you know."

The irony of that tasted bitter. "Just yours?" I asked.

76

"Hey! Back up. What's my agenda?"

"Two things so far," I said, rising to the bait despite myself. "One, you want to know whether Ed knows that David Thorne is Sid's father."

It was the faintest of tremors at the corner of her eyes, but it wiped my vision clean and I saw the significant issue. "Oh!" I said as she nodded encouragingly. "The question is, did Angele know. Would that give her a motive?"

Edith smiled. The pupil was slow, but she could add.

Edith still had a hooded look to her, predatory as a hawk. There was more. What did she see that I still didn't? My mind was going blank, circuits overcharging. I wondered hazily how many brain cells were dying as I looked at her, how many, at fifty-two I still had left.

"That's not an agenda," she prompted. "I could hardly . . . After all, we'd only just met. Anyway, it's Gram paying you, not me. It's her agenda I'd worry about if I were you."

Agenda. Edith's agenda had me feeling like a friggin' shuttle-cock batted between her and Ed. "It's Sid, isn't it?" I ventured.

Her eyes opened wide as a lantern. "Ah!" she breathed.

"Your agenda is to see no one railroads him." Another thought churned my remnant brain cells. "Who's his mother?" I asked.

"Jackie Soper?"

"I don't know. Does she have a sister? A half-sister?"

"Come to think of it, I believe she does. Why?"

I explained that my landlady, Nell St. John, was

Sid Soper's aunt, Jackie Soper's sister, and that Nell, too, was afraid Sid might be railroaded for David Thorne's murder. But Edith assured me, as Nell had done, that Sid had no idea David Thorne was his father, that David Thorne had been the rapist whose violence had blighted his mother's life and his own. She assured me, as Nell had done, that Sid had had no motive for murder.

"What makes you think," I asked, "that Ed wants to railroad Sid?"

"I didn't say that he does." She sounded exasperated.

"But if he does, you want to know it."

She nodded. "You got it."

"Well, I said, "I could live with that."

We thought our separate thoughts for a while. Then I said, "The other thing is it seems like a hornets' nest and I don't think I want to stir things up. No more'n I have already."

" 'Fraid you might get stung?"

"Damn right."

"Eyup. Can't say I blame you."

Then I asked what she made of the scene at the convent. "What's going on up there?" I asked. "Why did Gram Du Lac send me there?"

"You mean what agenda does that old lady have?"

"Yeah. She worries me."

"Good. You're not as dumb as you look."

"So, when I told Sr. Pat I was quitting, she begs me not to. Says Du Lac hates her. Is she a dyke?"

"Gram? I doubt it."

"Get outta here. Pat."

"Oh. There're rumors. But I don't put any store in them."

"Gossip?"

"Oh some of that too. Politicians and Religious, people always talk about 'em. Fact of life. But I don't believe it about Pat."

I waited to give her a chance to say, as conclusive evidence, something about Pat being a good person. But she didn't. I asked, "I gather there was something between her and Angele?"

"That I don't know anything about."

I laughed. "Not even gossip?"

"No, not even that."

Then it's probably not so, I thought.

After a while she said, "So you're quitting."

This woman was expert, but I was through jumping. "Yep. I think I'm in over my head."

"I can understand that. Are you going to see Ed yet tonight?"

"Soon as I do up these dishes."

"If, after you've seen him, you change your mind, I have a proposition for you."

I should have driven straight to Greenville. Instead, I said, "A proposition?"

"Yeah. But go see Ed first."

As I went out the door, she called after me. "There's a good movie on TV tonight. Check my light when you get back. If it's on, and you want, stop in."

The drive to Blue Hill from Surry is only fifteen minutes. But it was time enough for me to get into trouble.

We were close to the solstice. At 7:30 the sun was still high, the air muggy. I was in Ireland once at the solstice. It coincided with a full moon. As the sun, for hours, skimmed the arc of the horizon, light seemed to spring from the earth itself like a radiant gel.

I began to unwrap the bundle of emotions I had been carrying around with me since I'd tumbled into Ed's relationship with Angele, since this morning when I'd spent a lifetime precariously gazing into the troubled depths of Angele's eyes, of Angele's soul — as it then had seemed.

I felt left out. That was it. Standing alone — poorly clothed, ratty in fact — in the rain.

Brigid, you flying asshole!

Okay. Alone. Alone's okay. Alone looking through the window of a brightly lit house, seeing lots of people having a good time. Ed and Angele having a good time. And me, uninvited, nowhere to go, I stand there. Alone.

Poor me!

Poor me. So I follow it through. Step by dreary step. Trot down to the first liquor store. Lots of bright lights there. Nice and warm. Friendly man at the cash register. Pick up a bottle. Bottle under arm, run back, ring bell. Lovely house, lovely door, lovely Angele, jolly Ed. "Welcome, Brigid. Come on in. And aren't we having a great time!"

Say we don't have a fight. Say we get through the night still being jolly. Wake up now in the morning, the afternoon. In which room will it be?

The gorge of my disgust rose in my throat like the lump of vomit I did not need to taste; sweat filmed my upper lip and forehead. At the fairgrounds, I turned the car. With any luck I could make the eight o'clock meeting in Ellsworth and still have plenty of time afterwards to see Ed. Shouldn't go there without calling first anyway. Wasn't much I could ask Ed about Angele with her sitting right there with him.

As I found out later, Angele wasn't there. Couldn't have been. She was still sitting at the acre of glass wall looking out toward Spain. Dead.

The meeting was a step meeting. Fourth step. "Make a searching and fearless inventory of ourselves." Awright! Can do! Brigid Donovan's a flying asshole!

Someone named Mary spoke about how much harm we do beating ourselves up, that an inventory was just that, about good and bad, not just about what was missing but also about what was there. I'd made the meeting. I hadn't taken the drink. It was a nice place to start.

I called Ed a little after 9:00 p.m. from Ellsworth.

"Brigid! Love! Of course come over. Not at all. I'm all alone. And who would be with me? Wasn't I sitting here hoping you'd call!"

Old bag of mouse turds! I realized I *was* jealous. Of Ed! I got to laughing over it. Over myself. It was dusk, nearly dark, and the moon rising behind me most of the trip.

This time driving down, my thinking was more constructive. I ticked off the facts: David Thorne murdered. David Thorne, rapist. David Thorne, the father of Sid, a lost soul if ever there was one, lost and rather frightening. I thought of the people with motive strong enough, possibly, to drive them to murder. There was Jackie Soper, victim of the rape, whom I hadn't met yet. Then there was Sid, David's

81

son, Sid whom my new pal Edith and my old pal Nell were anxious to protect. The first question to be answered was, did Sid even know that David Thorne was his father? I would have to find out. I remembered Edith's hint: Did Angele — David Thorne's wife — know about the rape? Did she know about Sid? Perhaps I could find the answers to those questions from Ed. But even if Angele had known, after all those years would the motive be strong enough for murder? But first things first: Did Ed himself know that David Thorne was Sid Soper's father? I knew for sure that Sid's half-sister, the fragile Genevieve, did not know about their relationship. I remembered, as I turned up Ed's drive, that neither Sid nor Genevieve seemed to think much of Angele. I wondered why.

Ed was pretty far gone by the time I got there, but he seemed glad to see me.

"Brigid, I'd've never figured you for such a prude. What kind of an Irish lass are you? Have a drink for God's sake. It'll never hurt you."

I hadn't figured out yet how to get Ed to tell me whether he knew who Sid's father was. But I was pretty sure, as I had been with Angele earlier in the day, that he was operating in a blackout. I could ask him anything and it wouldn't make any difference in the morning. He wouldn't remember. And *in vino veritas*, which, strictly speaking, isn't true at all. But he was drunk enough that I could tell when he started to lie.

Showing him my bottle of coke, I said, "No. I've got all the drink I need right here, Ed. Thanks. Listen. I want to ask you a question."

"And I'm all ears."

82

"Who's Sid's father?"

"Ah, Brigid. It's you who're the detective, not your buddy, Ed Kelly. What is it you're doin' to earn that good bread?"

"I think it's David Thorne."

He winked at me and nodded solemnly. "Now, there's a bright girl. Let me freshen your drink."

Edith's light was on when I got back, but she wasn't watching television. She was waiting up for me.

"He knows," I said.

"Ah hah! That's interesting. So, do you want to hear my proposition?"

Chapter 9

It was a proposition all right, I thought wryly the next morning looking down on the blue black landscape of the Maine woods. In the distance, fading into the morning haze, lay the lighter blue of Penobscot Bay peppered with islands. The seventy-eight dollar Eastern Express is not the most comfortable way to get to New York City, it's eighteen seats crowded into a doll-size fuselage; and it's not the fastest, stopping here and there along the way. But you can't beat the price. For seventy-eight bucks, they bring you back again.

After I had recounted my conversation with Ed, which seemed to satisfy her, I said, "So you got a proposition for me."

She stared a while over my shoulder, in consultation perhaps with her Navy dad, who looked young and smart-alecky in a silver frame on her television.

"Let me test a few ideas I have, see what you think: First, it's extremely unlikely the state police will solve the murder."

Reflecting on the unsolved crimes I knew of since I'd moved to Maine, I thought she was probably right. No one had walked in on the murder in progress. Occurring as it did out in the woods, no neighbors had witnessed it, no one had heard it happening.

"There was no love lost between Gram Du Lac and David Thorne." She saw me hesitate on that one. Despite what Gen had said, I really did not know. "Take my word. She didn't exactly blame him for the mess Angele became, how could she. Still, in some way she seemed to hold him responsible. Maybe thought a real man would've straightened her out, wouldn't put up with it. Know what I mean? Not that she would've killed him, but more'n likely she'd think whoever did was doing God's work for Him. So that leaves a big question: Why's she paying good money, very good money, I might say, to you?"

"How do you know what she's paying me?"

Edith nibbled her bottom lip before saying, "We're getting closer to my proposition. Can we go at it my way and let that question lay for a minute? For right now, let's just say that I do know. It's darn good money. Now, what's she paying it for if it isn't to solve the crime?" She looked at me expectantly, not quite without patience: Brigid's slow, but she's getting there.

"Well, let's see," I said. But I preferred to follow my own train of thought for a moment. "You're a good friend of Sid's mother. What's her name, Jackie Soper. So I guess you found out what I'm getting paid through her. I told Nell. Nell told her sister, Jackie. Jackie told you. So . . . your question is: If Du Lac doesn't want me to solve the murder, what does she want. She probably wants me to set someone up. What Nell's afraid of. Is that what you think?"

"That's the way I have it figured," Edith agreed. "The only thing that bothers me, what I don't know, is who she intends to make the fall guy. My proposition to you is this: Stay on the case at least until you know who she has in mind for the rap. That's the first part. The second part's this: I'll collaborate with you free for nothing for as long as you want me to. Not my agenda." She wagged her finger at me. "All above board. I know these people. You don't. What do you think?"

Sounded terrific. I did have a little problem. A couple of them. No, three to be exact.

"For one thing Du Lac's paying me, like you said, very good money. It sounds more like I'd be working for you. I mean, you call it collaborating. But I don't think, somehow, I could call Du Lac tomorrow and tell her how lucky she is to be getting the two of us for the price of one. Know what I mean?"

"Oh yeah. You got a point. But what if you look at it this way: It seems to me there're two issues. One's how you act. There's nothing wrong with doing an honest investigation. Is there? It's what she hired you to do. She didn't offer you five hundred a week to frame someone. Did she? Of course not. The other issue is the money. Should you take the money if, regardless of what she says, you begin to suspect that's what she really wants you to do? If you quit now, she'll just hire someone else. And if you're really scrupulous, you can give the money to charity. H.O.P.E. for instance."

Made sense. She went on to deal just as neatly with my scruples regarding Sr. Pat and Nell.

"So long as your instructions are to investigate David's death and that's what you're doing, other people's agendas, as you call them, are just that. You might want to be careful about how you follow Gram's instructions, maybe avoid them. Be busy — don't go see her any more. And remember, you can give the money to charity. Or you can give it back."

I remembered enough canon law from a course I once took from Raymond de Roover to be comfortable with the idea of giving the money to charity. Once she'd settled my conscience, Edith outlined other plans for me. It took until nearly one o'clock. She'd thought it prudent — her word — to make reservations on the 9:55 a.m. Eastern Express to New York for me. She said Sid would take me to the airport so I wouldn't have to worry about the car.

Why New York?

"I've been thinking." Edith gestured at the yellow balls of foolscap littering the floor around her. "We could sort of lay back and react to whatever Gram sets in motion. Or we could try to get to the bottom of things ourselves. And I don't know about you, but I've always preferred the driver's seat myself. I never find the brakes on the passenger side work too good."

Sr. Pat, she said, wasn't going to let Gen alone

with me again. That she was sure of. Didn't I think it would be smart to talk with Gen's brother, Paul. There was something funny about those two kids. Always had been. She'd always thought so.

No longer having a large expense account for this investigation, I called an old friend, Erika Duncan, from the days I used to live in New York. Not only could she put me up, I'd caught her just as she was going out the door on her way to a ten-day lecture tour of the Southwest and California. I could pick up the key to her apartment from her doorman.

At La Guardia I caught the limo to Grand Central station. From there I took the shuttle across town to Times Square and the Seventh Avenue line going down to Fourteenth Street. I love to surface there by St. Vincent's Hospital. I remember when they built it for a maritime union, the lines of portholes giving it the appearance of an enormous concrete ship run aground in Greenwich Village. I'd packed light, fitting a couple changes of clothing in an army surplus backpack that belonged to one of the twins. I felt twenty-eight again, off on some assignation, some great adventure.

Hudson hummed. More happening at the intersection of Hudson and Bleeker Streets in a day than happened in all of Maine in a year, I thought happily, and I wondered, as I always do my first day or two in Manhattan, how can I bear to leave it? I stopped at D'Agostino's for a pound of Medaglia D'Oro and bagels. The doorman at West Beth gave me the key and a note from Erika welcoming me.

I hadn't been in her apartment for at least ten years, not since Judy Chicago's appearance there in the days when it was still the Women's Salon. Erika's artist husband, now former husband, had transformed their loft into a brightly painted sculpture. A breakfast nook, like a stage, overlooked the living area, and a curtained palanquin, arrested it seemed in mid-air above the common room sheltered their bed. His sculptures, her paintings, paintings and drawings by their children, adorned walls and other surfaces. Books lay everywhere. Nef, the elegant Siamese, greeted me with a long and thoughtful catalogue of complaints. I commiserated, had days like that myself, while I looked for the Manhattan phone book.

Found it, finally, on the fridge under a thirsty begonia. Watered the plant and moved it nearer the light. Couldn't find a listing for Emmaus. I felt a qualm about arriving unannounced, unlooked for at 124th and Lexington, in the heart of Harlem. But it wasn't to be helped. Edith and I had agreed we didn't want to alert anyone in Maine of what I was doing.

We had agreed that if she hadn't heard from me by eleven that evening, Edith was to call in the cavalry. It had seemed reassuring last night, the thought of a backup there in Maine. Today, in a suddenly bleaker Manhattan, it seemed to signify small comfort, a shorter stay, perhaps, in a cooling tray at the morgue, a tag on my toe, Female Caucasian. I was beginning to remember how it was I always managed to tear myself away from Manhattan when it was time to go.

Chapter 10

From 110th Street on, I was the only white in the subway car. No one else seemed to notice. At 125th, at the top of the stairs, two young men in spotless white robes sold literature on Islam, the crowds breaking respectfully around them, some dropping coins in the bowl on their table, murmuring a greeting.

Above ground it was hot, the kind of heat only the city generates, rising from the sun-baked pavement, pouring from exhausts and the simmering radiators of traffic-stalled busses and cars, trapped among the buildings, caught in a translucent veil of sun-riveted molecules. Manhattan-hot.

I hadn't been to Harlem in nearly twenty years. It looked as if they'd had a war. One block was nothing but rubble, reminding me of Derry and Belfast when Ed and I visited there. Half the remaining buildings were gutted. As in Derry and Belfast, the people seemed not to notice. If the war had been against poverty, poverty had won hands down.

I took my bearings and headed down Lexington to 124th Street. There was no sign for the Emmaus Hotel. But my choices were limited: on the uptown east side of the street was the block of rubble, on the west an unpromising building with a bodega and two vacant store fronts on the ground floor. Across the street, a bombed out building that appeared to be deserted, in fact the local crack house; I hoped to God it wasn't my destination. That left a five-story building on the downtown east side. I crossed over. It had one entrance, a red metal door facing onto Lexington.

Two men sat on the stairs sharing a bottle of Thunderbird wrapped in a paper bag. "Afternoon, Sister," one, from the islands, said.

"Afternoon. Is this the Emmaus Hotel?"

He got unsteadily to his feet and rang the bell. "Yes, Sister. Sure is."

"Do you live here?" I asked as we waited.

"Oh no." He scrubbed a spot above his ear. His chino pants, no longer shiny, were stained and frayed. A knotted rope kept them from falling off his wasted frame. His undershirt, except for a fresh splash of wine beneath his left nipple, like an archipelago of blood, the Antilles from where he came, was clean and new looking.

"They has too many rules. Eddy and I, we live next door." He waved his bottle toward the block of rubble and giggled. Eddy appeared to have fallen asleep. "But we eats our dinners hyar. We dine out mos' nights."

The metal door opened. The young man, light-skinned, good-looking, said, "John!" his tone exasperated, but loving, the father about to reprimand, his heart not really in it.

"It is too hot at home," John protested. "This hyar step's the only cool place around. Besides, Eddy and me want to be first in line for dinner."

"You and Eddy could live here . . ."

"Aw, you don't want us, boss." He bent and shook Eddy awake. "Eddy, come walk wit me now."

"Sister?" the young man looked at me and asked.

"Hello. I'm not a Sister. I'm looking for Paul Thorne."

"I'm Paul."

Genevieve was right. He could pass in Harlem. He just had. I don't think I managed to mask my surprise. I said, "I met your sister yesterday. She said you were like twins."

"Oh? You must be from Maine. How is Gen?"

"Okay. I guess. Could I come in?"

Eddy and John moved off the step and on down the block. Paul opened the door wide for me. "Do you know about Emmaus?" he asked.

The small tiled entrance opened on either side into a hall. Before us rose a wide staircase. The stucco walls, painted white, smelled clean, of fresh

92

cement. Above us, on the white wall of the landing hung an icon, boldly painted, the style so Eastern it took me a moment to recognize the "saint." It was Dorothy Day.

"Emmaus? Well, it's the town where Jesus met the disciples. Is that what you mean? After the resurrection?"

"Oh. Right. I meant the Emmaus Movement. Like the Hotel and all."

I didn't. But I soon found out. His enthusiasm, like his sister's laugh, was infectious. He seemed more of this world than Genevieve, but there was about him also a hint of that ethereal peace. I was on my guard not to shatter it.

"Abbé Pierre started it after World War Two, he and a man who'd tried to commit suicide. Everything seemed so hopeless, then they met, and I guess it was like what happened at Emmaus, when Jesus came and the disciples got inspired. So they gathered a bunch of homeless people together, and there were a lot after the war 'n all, like here now, and they picked the dumps. That's how they made a living. And they built homes. They got to be called the rag pickers of Paris. Now there're hundreds of places, all around the world, like this."

I knew about picking dumps. It was a living. But buying Manhattan real estate? I wondered what they dumped in Paris and if it could be legal to find it. I murmured politely.

Paul took me up to his room on the fifth floor. Small and austere, it held only two pieces of furniture, an iron cot made with army-like precision, and a battered bureau painted, like the walls, a flat white. On the bureau a cardboard frame held a picture, black and white, of Gen in her habit, and beside it, the only spot of color in the room, lay a red Lectionary with gold lettering. It was hot in there, the air too still. The smell of paint and cement had begun to nauseate me.

"You okay?" Paul asked. "We could go up on the roof. There's shade, and a breeze usually. You can tell me about Gen."

On the roof, the patches of shade were small but growing larger. A boardwalk ran from the stairwell around the perimeter of the roof. We sat with our backs to the parapet on the Lexington side. The traffic sounds were muted up there and the breeze felt good, but the air was rank with diesel fumes and the pungent odor of melting tar.

"How is Gen?" he asked once we were settled. He had offered to run down for some newspaper to sit on. The boardwalk was grimy with soot. But I had said my jeans had seen worse. His overalls were paint-stained and dusty with plaster. His hair, faintly orange, grew full on his head like a helmet. He seemed fidgety and, as we sat there — me stunned by the heat and mesmerized by the syncopated rhythm of the distant traffic — he glanced several times at his watch.

I began by explaining that I had met Gen only the day before. Then I asked, "Am I keeping you from something?"

He said, "Oh, it's nothing. I promised to meet a friend up here. He's late. That's all."

But he seemed to slow down some inside. He said, "I haven't seen Gen since she's been in the convent."

"Convent!" I said. "Have you seen pictures of it?"

"No. But Gen's told me. I know it's nothing fancy."

"I upset her," I said abruptly, surprising myself.

"You upset her?"

Defensively, I said, "I didn't mean to. I just told her I had been to visit her mother . . ."

Like Gen, Paul became disturbed. "Our mother? Angele? When was that?"

"Yesterday," I said, "but it seems more like a year ago."

"What happened?" he demanded, pushing his face close to mine. The pupils of his eyes were like dark, hard stones, fossils in a sea of amber.

I said, "She started to scream."

"Who started to scream?"

"Who? Gen."

"Why?" he asked, his voice harsh, his breath sour. "What did you do to her?"

I rushed to justify myself. "I didn't do anything. I just said, 'I visited your mother this morning.' I described Gen's surprising response.

"I raised my hand to calm her," I explained. "That's when she started to scream. Pat, the other nun, accused me of abusing her."

"Abusing her?"

His face turned gray in the shadow of the parapet. He grabbed my shoulder. "She said you abused her?"

"No!" I cried. "You're hurting me. I don't know what she said. She was angry. That's all."

"Tell her, Paul."

Paul broke away. Like a spring uncoiling, he leaped to his feet.

The newcomer stood, nonchalant as Michelangelo's David, before us. His hand lay gracefully touching the black bikini draped across his loins; his skin, like David's, was bronze. I wondered how much of his posture was self-conscious. He was beautiful.

"You're late, man!" Paul's breath was short, as if he'd been running.

"Get outta here!" the young man said. "Late! It's summer, man! Hey! We got held up in traffic. You gonna introduce me to your friend?"

"Oh, sure. Sorry. Uh. I forgot your name," Paul said to me.

I was on my feet, away from the parapet, closer to the door, my hand out. "Brigid Donovan. From Maine."

"Ralph Light here," the newcomer said. "Glad to meet you, Sister. You from Gen's convent?"

"I'm not a Sister. I'm from Gen's grandmother, actually," I explained, stretching the truth.

"Gram! How is she?"

"Mrs. Du Lac? You know her?"

"Yeah, I met her," Ralph said.

Paul Thorne was getting fidgety again.

Continuing to edge my way toward the door, I kept the conversation going by asking, "You from Maine, too?"

Ralph sidled along beside me. I could see the pearls of sweat nestling among the forest of golden hairs on his arms and chest. He said, "Sure am. Me and Paul, here, we're practically brothers." He laughed. Laughed too hard. I gained the door. "Oh yes?" I said, politely.

"Yep. Both born in Ellsworth. Same hospital and

everything. Paul was born in sixty-four. And I was born in sixty-five. What do you think about that?" Think about it? Not much. "Well, isn't that interesting," I said. "So, you've known each other like all your life?"

I entered the stairwell. Ralph held the door for me. Paul, behind me, seemed uninterested in our conversation, seemed interested only in Ralph, was following Ralph. But Ralph, who continued to hover at my side, seemed oddly interested. He seemed to savor what he was telling me; the information he imparted to me seemed to please him. He had more.

"Oh, no. We just met this summer. Here at Emmaus. I grew up in California. Except for getting born in Maine, I've never been East before. Not till last month. I got here about four weeks ago."

At the landing, Ralph turned to Paul. "Why don't you stay on the roof. I'll show the Sister out and bring us back a couple beers."

He took my elbow. I tried not to flinch.

"He gets upset easy," said Ralph as Paul retreated out of sight and hearing.

"Yeah. So does his sister."

"Yeah. Well. Maybe they got reason to."

I wondered whether he intended to tell me about it. He seemed to debate something in his head. I wondered what he had meant when he said to Paul up on the roof, "Tell her!"

"I'd like to know," I prompted.

He said, "Look. could we meet? Later, you know, tonight, away from here?"

"Sure," I said. "I'm staying down in the Village. At a friend's apartment."

"Be better some place private. So we could talk."

We were standing by then on the last landing. "Saint" Dorothy looked on impassively, her face outlined in gold and black and deep magenta. Ralph Light stood so close I could feel the heat of his skin on mine. He smelled of fresh sweat and sun oil. The faint stubble of beard on his cheek was yellow like the hair springing in tight Medusa curls about his face. He radiated sensuality and I felt myself warm to it. Talk about resurrection.

"I mean, you alone there? Or what?"

I said yes without thinking, and then, regretting it, added lamely a lie: "Well, not exactly. But we'll be private." He looked doubtful so I improvised. "I mean, it's a double loft, down at West Beth. I'm staying in half of it, at a friend's. She's not there. The other person's downstairs. It's real private. Really. What time can you come?"

"Can I buzz you?"

I gave him the number. He said he would call around 10:30 or a little after.

I called Edith at one minute past 11:00, not having heard yet from Light, as I had come to think of him. I had an early supper in the apartment, this and that from a deli: Genoese salami, three kinds of salad, Italian bread, all crust and sweet butter. After Maine and the IGA a real treat. Then I rode uptown again to the Thalia and sat through two Fellini flicks. One, *Americord*, I had never seen. I got back just before 11:00, confident that if Light had called, he would call again.

But when the doorbell rang at ten after, I was both surprised and alarmed. I was sure it was him. What disturbed me was nobody knowing he was in the building, not even Edith. I wondered how he got past the doorman.

I must have been expecting him to arrive in his black bikini and white towel because I felt a letdown opening the door to find him looking rather ordinary in khaki slacks and a blue polo shirt, an alligator crawling across the pocket.

"I thought you'd call."

"Is your friend here?"

"She's in Albuquerque. Oh, you mean the roommate. As a matter of fact, I think she's reading." I gestured to the closed door behind me. "Come on in." We climbed the stairs to the upper part of the apartment.

"What's this thing?" he asked, pointing upward as we passed under the palanquin.

"Nothing. Just decorative," I lied, not wanting him to know, for some reason, where I slept.

"Paul says you're not a Sister."

"That's right."

"For some reason I thought you were. That you, uh, came from Gen's convent."

"No."

"The way you were questioning Paul. I thought."

"Actually, I wasn't questioning him. I'd wanted to. It was more like he was questioning me." And I repeated once again the incident with Gen at the convent. By this time I had the sequence down pat. "She got excited, I mean really upset, when I mentioned her mother's name. But she didn't start screaming till I raised my hand. Like this." And I raised my right hand, extending it toward him as if I intended to stroke the furry hair, soft and golden, of his forearm.

"That's interesting," he said. And I drew back my hand, locking the wrist securely in the clasp of the other one, thumb pressed tight over my pulse.

"You said, up on the roof, 'Tell her, Paul.' " I asked, "What was that about?"

"Right!" He jumped up and began to pace the small oval of floor between couch and desk, hands thrust deep in the pockets of his pants, chin touching the fold of his collar. His attention seemed focused on his feet, leather thong sandals, his arch high and delicate, the second toe longest, gold hairs springing from each knuckle.

"You said Mrs. Du Lac sent you. Why is that?"

"She's concerned. About Gen. About the father's murder. She wanted me to see her. It was my idea to come to New York. I thought Paul might understand what that was all about at the convent. I mean, something's really wrong there. Frankly, I think Gen could use some professional help."

"Yeah." He sat down again, on the edge of the chair, his body turned toward me, his knees nearly touching mine. "Can I trust you?" he asked. His eyes, the color of amber, not much darker than his hair, almost the same glowing bronze as his skin, contained lighter flecks, like agate.

"How do you mean trust?"

"I guess I'm not clear what your motives are."

My first thought: *you're* not clear? My second was, *my* motives? This young man was used to getting his way, and I hadn't a clue what he was after.

100

"My motives are to help if I can, and to prevent more harm." Not too clear, maybe, but true.

"Yeah. Well. I don't know how much you want to tell the grandmother. Paul tells me she's getting up there. I think a lot of this goes way back. You know, I was brought up Catholic too. And, uh, I mean I don't go to church or anything. But, you know, that stuff sticks."

Tell me about it.

"Like, not that you can go to confession or anything like that. Still, paying a shrink seventy-five bucks an hour. For what a priest did. Cause really, you think about it, it's the same thing. Isn't it? Sure it is. The shrink says it's all potty training and your mother's fault. The priest calls it original sin. But they both forgive you. So what's the difference? Really. You know what I mean?"

Yeah. I'd heard the line before. In AA we call it the Fifth Step. "Admitted to God, to ourselves and to another human being the exact nature of our wrongs." You pays your money and you picks your poison. I nodded, not too encouragingly.

"Well, what I was thinking's this. My dad knew the Thornes. The two families were real tight. Country club, all that kind of stuff. He's in Boston. Seems to me, he might be able to help. Like, you know, in college I took some psych courses. That stuff starts young. One prof I had said it's all over by the time you're two. I mean like two's stretching it. It's more like one, or whenever it was you got potty trained. Anyway, my dad knew the Thornes back then when Gen and Paul were babies. I mean really knew the family. Intimate's the word. See,

Gen's two years older'n me. And I was almost three when we moved to California. So, anyway I just thought it might help talking to him."

"Sure. That's a good idea." Uh, how do I go about it?"

"Well, hey, what if I give him a ring tomorrow. Tell him you're coming. Ask when he can see you. You know, like set it up?"

"Good. Terrific. Hey, thanks a lot," I heard myself say. Talking that way is, like, catching, you know?

We left it that he'd call me in the morning, let me know what his dad said.

"Your friend's awfully quiet," Ralph said as we passed the downstairs bedroom on the way to the door.

"Must've gone to sleep."

Edith called as I closed the door on him. I was out of breath by the time I answered.

She began with no preliminaries. "I had the scanner on. You sitting down? You sound out of breath."

"I am. Sitting down and out of breath. What's up?"

"Your friend Angele."

"She's not my friend."

"She's not anybody's friend. She's dead."

"What!"

"Yep. Neighbor found her. Hadn't heard from her. Let himself in. Found her about nine or so tonight evidently. Been dead a while. Like they say, you might've been the last person to see her alive."

Chapter 11

Ralph Light's father wanted to take me to lunch at the Harvard Club!

"Come on," I protested.

"That's the kind of dude he is," Ralph Light assured me. "Treats his kids the same way. Last of the big spenders. That's the good news. And I won't bother you with the bad, like the eighteen grand I owe for a two-bit education. Anyway —"

"What time?"

It was seven. His ring had awakened me. The news about Angele had left me sleepless, tossing in my sweaty sheets in the palanquin, until after four. I felt tired and grumpy. He sounded fresh and young and still beautiful.

"Anytime. You call him when you get there."

"You coming back to New York, Sister?"

"Is that sister-friend or sister-nun?"

"Does it matter?"

"I guess not." I let my irritation show.

"If it bothers you."

"It does kind of."

"Do my best. You coming back?"

"I guess so. Ralph, I heard some terrible news last night . . ."

"I know. I found out when I got back here."

"How's Paul taking it?"

"Not so good. He's left for Maine. In fact his plane's about to take off right this minute."

How to get to Boston was a problem. And what to do with Erika's key. Decided to keep the key. If I didn't return that evening I could always mail it to her. I couldn't afford to fly, could hardly afford the bus. On the other hand, I could fly on plastic. The bus wanted bills. I showered, dressed and started out for Grand Central Station, crossroads of the world, etc.

I had to wait fifteen minutes for the shuttle. Everyone else was all dressed up, the men, despite the heat, in three-piece suits, the women in heels. Rapees is how I think of them, teetering around, throwing their backs out, disabled by skirts too tight to run, unable to defend themselves. A blinking neon light couldn't advertise their vulnerability more clearly: Victim. Victim. Victim. I wished, however, that my own shoes didn't have those fraying holes by my little toes. My canvas shoes always wear out there. I never remember to notice whether other people have the same problem. Sometimes I think it's my toes. Sometimes I think it's the manufacturer's fault. Other than the shoes I wasn't too disreputable. My jeans were clean and my shirt was okay.

Come on, Brigid! Harvard Faculty Club? Jeans, torn deck shoes. Maybe when I called him we could arrange to meet somewhere else. Take-out. Sit on the grass. More private, you know. Yeah.

Sometimes I get to looking around for some other fifty-two year-old lady, hair almost white, shaggy but clean, jeans, tennis shoes with little holes starting where the toes begin on the side there, just to see how I think she looks. Except for the time I caught sight of myself unexpectedly in a store mirror, I've never seen one. I thought I looked okay. But you can't tell, just once like that and no time to study her, it being me and all, and if I'd stopped to stare it would have been like looking at myself in the mirror at home. Except I don't have a mirror. Nell does in her bathroom, but I don't like to ask to use it. It sounds like I'm being vain. It's hard to explain I'm just curious.

They said it wasn't as hot in Boston. Maybe so. But between ninety and ninety-four is not such a big deal. The pilot said it was unusually hot for this time of year. He said if we were going on to Maine it was cooler there, only seventy but raining.

I got to the square at half past eleven, too early for lunch. I walked up to the Fogg and discovered they were charging admission. There's a Botticelli in the Fogg I always go to see. It's like a visit with her really, Madonna holding her child, the fingers of her hand so sensuous, the tortured sensuality reflected also in her eyes, so serene on the surface but like Angele's eyes, like Genevieve's, the surface a thin cover over unimaginable depths where dragons lurk and I long to follow. I decided to give it a pass and people-watch in the yard instead. At one I called him.

It has come to seem to me that I solved the case the moment I laid eyes on Ralph Light's father. That's not really true, though. At that moment I was only dumbfounded. And I didn't really understand it all for some weeks to come. but it may be true that my subconscious grasped it all in that moment when I first saw him, and that it took the extra weeks simply for my conscious mind to catch up and fill in the holes my intuition had leaped over. What I did know instantly, with no doubt at all, was that Jimmy Light — not David Thorne — was Paul Thorne's father. That is what I had been sent to see.

Coming out of the yard, I spotted him lounging outside the door of the Club. If I said Harry Bellafonte, you'd get the idea of how Africa and Europe had come together in Jimmy Light. The bone structure of his face northern, Celtic perhaps, fine, the bridge of his nose high, hooked even. His hair, trimmed close to his skull, was slightly grizzled above his ears, but seemed for the most part to be the same almost orange color as his son's, as Malcolm X's. And like Malcolm's too was the mottled high color of his skin.

He was tall and lean, wearing a seersucker jacket, shirt open at the throat, and blue linen slacks. His loafers were the kind with two tassels. I didn't think he'd be too happy walking into the Harvard Faculty Club with me on his arm. Neither could I see him cross-legged on the grass in front of Widener. He shot back his cuff to look at the time. I was ten minutes late. Screw it! I turned right and trotted off toward the T. If he saw me, he'd think it was just another old lady jogging. It *was* just another old lady jogging!

At the airport I discovered I would save almost fifty dollars returning to Maine by way of New York. I was feeling so totally demoralized by my indecision, or wrong decision — either way, I felt like a klutz — I didn't begin to focus on the implications of what I'd found out until I was slouched in the corner of my seat crossing the bridge in from Queens. It was 5:00 p.m. and the traffic coming from Manhattan was something out of *Brazil*. Maybe it was my reaction to seeing all those people, almost all of them alone, isolated inside a ton or so of steel and plastic, fighting each other to get where, Queens? Long Island? I don't know, but as the limo turned downtown, my mood lightened. I stopped beating on myself. I'd found out what I was meant to. A two martini lunch in the HFC before I'd had time to think the new information through would probably have gained me nothing but heartburn. Safe inside Manhattan, I sort of wished I'd gone ahead with it, my mind bright with the fantasy of my approach, Jimmy Light seeing through me, waiting for the black garbed nun, then his face as he came to terms with me.

Since I'd saved so much money coming back to New York instead of going straight home, I decided I could afford to go out to dinner. Decisions like that have made it impossible for me to buy my own piece of paradise in Maine.

I looked around for a while trying to find a place

107

I used to go. Old men played Bocci in the back. Couldn't find it. Passed by the building Alger Hiss used to live in and my old drinking buddy, Dina. They took her a couple of times to St. Elizabeth's with the DTs. She had a problem, I thought back then. She drank a quart of vodka daily, buying the next day's bottle in the late afternoon, breaching it each morning when she got up. Never drunk. But the DTs were bad. Real bad. Lost touch with her years ago. For the hell of it, I went into the foyer and looked at the names. Hers wasn't there. Recovering? I wondered. Or dead?

After Alicia and I moved to Maine, she had her second encounter with the little green men and the spiders running up and down her arms. They took her to BMHI — the Bangor Mental Health Institute. When she got out, she moved back to Chicago. She had family there. We kept in touch, for a while. Then she moved to California. I often wonder what happened to her, whether she was a bag lady, maybe, in the Mission. I thought of her and Dina together, sharing a cardboard box for shelter. The thought was infinitely depressing.

I finally stopped at a little Italian place on Bleeker, one with specials, nothing fancy, families there with kids. I played safe with a favorite, manicotti. Too much sauce, but it was good and I never make it myself. No way to compare, to regret, afterwards, the bill: $11.00 including tip. Not so bad.

I passed on dessert, intending to stop at D'Agostino's on my way back to Erika's. A chocolate croissant for tonight and a plain one for breakfast. Sounded good.

I called Edith when I got in. "What's the news about Angele?"

"Not much. Wasn't even in the paper this morning. Found her too late last night. On the evening news what they said, Ed — Oh, did I tell you it was Ed who found her?"

"Ed! No. You said it was a neighbor."

"I know. Well, on the scanner last night, that's what they were saying. But it was Ed apparently."

"Have you talked to him?"

"Yes. In fact I've got a message for you. He wants you to call him. He was on a crying jag. Wanted his 'darlin' girl.' I told him his 'darlin' girl' was probably asleep and maybe it could wait until morning."

"Edith, how did Angele die?"

"Messy. Like David."

"Oh, God. I really liked her."

"I know. Listen. She didn't suffer. They say she was pretty anesthetized. Now, enough of that. What did you find out?"

"I found out David Thorne was not Paul Thorne's father."

"Come again?"

"Have you ever met Paul?"

"I've seen him. There was a tar brush somewhere, if that's what you mean."

"Yeah. That's what I mean. But this Jimmy Light I went to see in Boston. He's Paul's father. I'm sure of it."

"He just tell you that? I'm Paul Thorne's real father?"

"Didn't need to."

"Oh! He's colored."

"Yeah. But fair-skinned like Paul. They look a lot alike actually. What's even more interesting is that Paul's friend, Ralph, Ralph Light, wanted me to know about it."

"What's his game?"

"Wish I knew."

I'd no sooner hung up when the phone rang. It was Ralph Light. "What happened, Sister? Dad said you never showed."

Did you ask did he see a little old lady snaking down the street wearing gym shoes and jeans? "I think I didn't have to talk with him to get the message."

The silence was like a pothole in the road between us, getting bigger by the second. I gritted my teeth, determined not to fill it.

"You still there, Sister?"

"Ralph, I'm not your sister."

"Don't be touchy. Hey, he was really pissed. I mean, you call and say meet me in half-an-hour and you never show. I don't get it. Now you say you were there. I just don't get it."

"Ralph!"

"What."

"Look, it's obvious you and Paul Thorne are half brothers, and I think that's what you sent me to Boston to find out . . . No, wait, let me finish. I didn't feel prepared to talk about it then. And I'm not sure I know what to say now. Next time you talk to your dad, tell him I'm sorry. I really am."

"You done?"

"Yes, I'm done."

"Let me ask you one question. Do Paul Thorne and I look like half brothers?"

Click.

Hmmm. Good question. I even knew the answer. It was no.

Chapter 12

Next day I blew a ritual kiss down at the city:
Bye bye, Manhattan. We flew too far north for me to
make out West Beth. But I saw Central Park and the
lake. In the Bad Olde Days, the twins and I lived on
Central Park West. We moved there when I left
Heidi. The kids would visit her on weekends, across
the river in Brooklyn Heights. They still had their
own rooms in the apartment there.

It was a disappointing time. I'd found Rosemary
in a bar that first summer. The next summer, in
another bar, I lost her. That year of bar-hopping

seemed, at the time, like the youth I had mislaid in a convent, two pregnancies, and two stifling marriages. That's how I thought of the earnest four years I spent with Heidi. An overachiever herself, Heidi expected command performances from us all, and got them. The twins skipped a grade. I got my ABD (all but dissertation) from NYU, and, on the strength of that and the promise of a dissertation on 13th century Venetian guilds, I landed a job at Brooklyn College.

The years at Brooklyn College, too, were disappointing. Without Heidi to goad me, I didn't get much done on my Venetian guilds. I was faculty adviser of the W.E.B. Du Bois Club at Brooklyn College, but it was SDS that was igniting campuses across the country. A student, veteran of the House Un-American Activities Committee, came by one Saturday afternoon to ask me to join the newly organized Progressive Labor Party. He said I had a good class line. When I told him I was queer, he put down his beer and left. We didn't know then that the personal is political, but experiences like that told me something. Alicia moved in about then. Over Heidi's protests, and the twins'. Alicia is a journalist — how I met Ed Kelly, how I got into writing some myself. That time Alicia had the DTs was a weekend, and the kids were with Heidi.

We moved to Maine the year of the Columbia riots. So I missed Stonewall. Except for those first hours of madness whenever I visit Gotham, I've never regretted our decision to leave New York for Maine.

Sid was waiting in front of the airport at the wheel of my car, a beat-up old Toyota, mostly red. The door of the passenger side — I picked it up in a yard in Veazie after a drunk sideswiped me a couple years ago — was yellow. My favorite color, so I never painted it. Sid didn't return my greeting. I stowed my gear in the trunk and walked around to the driver's side. He kept on looking straight ahead as if I weren't there. I leaned down and spoke in his ear. It was well-formed. He was a good looking man. Too bad he was so weird.

"Shall I drive?"

He said, "Edith told me to pick you up, so get in."

Short of a major scene, I didn't see how to get him to move over. So I said, "Right!" and did what I was told.

"I should have warned you," Edith said. She thought it was funny. I still felt aggrieved. "Sid's always loved to drive, and of course he almost never gets a chance to."

Made sense and, letting go the tatters of my resentment, I became generous. "Maybe I could let him borrow my car sometime."

"Oh, I wouldn't."

"Why not? He seems like a good driver. Does he drink?"

"No, it's not that. He's afraid of you." Edith was amused. "He thinks you're weird. That's what he said."

We were sitting on her porch. The air was sweet with lilacs, the flowers of the bush beside her house the deep purple kind. A busy pair of robins hopped about the lawn, scouring it for worms, and Beatrice, the pregnant Holstein, browsed nearby as if she wanted company. I savored it. "I'm weird. Okay."

"Pour us a cup of coffee," said Edith, "and I'll tell you a story."

The story began over thirty years before. It had a quality of Walt Disney at the beginning. But it was more like Ambrose Bierce by the end. Life imitating art, but badly.

Angele Du Lac was the princess, the foundling. Born poor, child of servants and Quebecoise is at that — Frogs. A frog child. But astonishingly beautiful. It wasn't true that she swept the hearth. She was no Cinderella. But neither was it probable that she would marry a prince. Yet that is just about what she had done.

The wedding, in June, the lilacs were in bloom, took place on the estate where Angele grew up. It seemed Angele was the acknowledged daughter of the house. The prince by taking her hand had realized her true identity. She wasn't a frog at all. Not really. She was a WASP.

The party afterwards went on all night. On the lawn, in the tents and the heated pool, in the big house with the many rooms, with the many bedrooms. Some said it got out of hand. Edith left a little after midnight and as far as she was concerned it was out of hand already.

Edith in those days worked at the Country Club as a cook, helping her husband to eke out a meager living for their family. The Club catered the wedding with Edith supervising in the kitchen of the estate. She had procured for her sixteen year-old niece, Jackie, a job helping out. Jackie had never seen anything like it, had never imagined anything like it. No television then to feed her imagination with pictures. No movies even, not on the Island. And her folks didn't read much, just the newspapers occasionally, so there weren't books around. To Jackie the wedding and the party were like a fairy tale. Everything she saw that night was part of the happy ending and was desirable. She desired it. There was no thinking it through. It was sheer emotion, glitz, glamor. A child, or a fool, could have told her the prince only gets to rescue once. But she didn't need to be told. She knew that. It didn't stop her sixteen-year-old heart from longing to become the princess in a fairy tale of her own.

The happy couple left that night on a fairy tale honeymoon visiting castles in Ireland and France, in Luxembourg and Spain. They sent Angele's parents picture postcards of each palace, castle and chateau they visited and these Claire Du Lac gave to Edith to bring to Jackie who pinned them to the wall beside her bed where she could gaze at them at night before she went to sleep. All night long she would wander through them in dreams she hardly remembered.

The happy couple arrived back on the Island the first week in September. The welcome home party was held at the Country Club. In Edith's opinion, Angele and David were drunk when they got there.

"Not messy drunk," she explained. "Too young. Could still hold their liquor then. Both of them. But they had a snoot full. Believe me. The two of them."

She had once again got a job for Jackie helping out. "She was star struck. You know what I mean? Dazzled. She was just a kid, an innocent sixteen-year-old kid.

"I lost track of her. Things got pretty wild along about midnight. I expected it, after the wedding, and

I told Jackie she had to get her sweet patootie out of there by eleven. She had school the next day anyway, so I didn't have to spell it out. So when she disappeared, I just figured she'd gone home like I told her to."

Edith paused, her eyes turned back on that long-ago scene. "I got out of there about midnight. Next morning, knock on the door, six-thirty maybe. It was Ida, Jackie's ma. 'Sorry to get you up,' she says. 'Jackie with you?' I'm half asleep, standing there in my nightie, and I say, 'Yes.' She says, 'Just checking. Go back to bed.' And I did.

"But you know how it is. The words kept repeating themselves in my head till all of a sudden I woke up. Wait a minute! Jackie's not with me! So I climbed out of bed, dressed, went back to the club. There's a little gazebo there by the water. Used to be. Burned down the next summer and they never replaced it. I don't know why, but I made a bee-line for that gazebo.

"She was there all right. She was a sight. Clothes torn, hardly a stitch on her, and it was cold. She was in shock, hypothermia. I think if I'd been any later, we'd've lost her."

Edith shook her head at the memory and then related how she had wrapped Jackie in her coat and gone for help. A friend with a lobster boat took Jackie across to the hospital in Ellsworth.

"We were afraid to take her to the Island hospital. It was obvious what had happened. Her thighs were bruised and there was lots of blood, you know, down there. On the boat going over I washed her best I could. It's bad enough these days, but back then a girl got raped, people treated her like a

117

criminal. If you were lucky, no one ever knew. And I figured, well, let's face it, it had to of been someone at the party. That meant a Daddy with bucks. Big bucks. If Jackie said rape, even hinted at it, she would be in for big trouble."

They needn't have worried. The hospital attendants treated Jackie with indifference, as if treating girls in her condition was routine. Perhaps it was. The next day Jackie confided her story to Edith.

"She didn't realize he was drunk and when he asked her to go with him, to see the tide come in, or whatever foolishness he said, she went. And she let him kiss her. So she thought it must of been her fault what happened. But you could see how she'd struggled. He didn't mess her up like that for the hell of it. And she said she fought him to the end. When it was over he just got up and walked away. Left her like we found her."

Edith kept Jackie until the bruises faded. Told Jackie's ma that she had the measles. "That way I could keep the lights dim. No one could see the state she was in.

"When it became apparent that Jackie was pregnant, the school kicked her out. Her ma wanted to know who the father was. "But Jackie wasn't telling nobody," said Edith. "Too bitter and too scared. Jackie never got over it. She never finished school. Had to grow up overnight, having the baby and then having the care of it. Never had a chance to be young. And her family kicked her out. She stayed with us till the baby was born. Then she went over to Stockton Springs and lived with Nell for a while."

When Edith had begun her tale, she had begun to knit. The unidentifiable strip of multicolored yarn had grown into a mitten. She laid it down with a sigh. "Golly! I haven't told that story for years. Come to think of it, I don't think I ever told it! Are you hungry?" she suddenly asked. "I am."

I told her I'd picked up some bagels, cream cheese and hard salami in the village that morning. Over it she said, "Well, I guess what I've told you about Jackie was only the first chapter. Until today I thought it was the whole story."

What Edith told me next was based partly on fact and partly on deduction. You didn't need to be a Watson to agree with her conclusions.

Jackie's labor had been long and exhausting. Edith had been allowed to stay with her. Other women in the labor room came and went. One of them was Angele.

"When Jackie saw her, she tightened right up. She was holding my hand and it's a wonder I still have it left. What a bitter moment it must have been. I'm sure Angele didn't even recognize us. Not then. But later on she did and I think she put two and two together. Thought so then, sure of it now."

A day or two later, while Jackie and Edith were looking at little Sid through the nursery window, David and Angele appeared. They had come to admire Gen.

"David looked at Jackie, then, surprised like, he looked over to the baby. I don't know that it clicked. But Angele took in that look and she knew."

Edith's speculation continued. One of the young people in the Thorne's set was a girl from Philadelphia named Gladys Wells. She'd managed to cause a *real* scandal. She up and married a Black man, someone she'd met at Stanford, Jimmy Light.

119

Edith reasoned that Angele had gotten back at David by making his horns as public as she knew how, not caring whether she got pregnant by Jimmy Light, even hoping perversely that she might. "Wasn't she afraid of repercussions?" I asked. "I mean, it seems to me her own position among those people wasn't any too secure."

"What'd she care? Those were the good old days of alimony. I don't think she gave a good harumph. That older generation, scandal was worse than the bubonic plague to them. She could've written her own ticket, provided it was to some place far away. Who knows? Maybe that's what she wanted.

"If so, it didn't work. No one batted an eye. A real case of the Emperor's New Clothes. If old man Thorne grins and says how the baby's the spittin' image of his granddaddy, who's gonna tell him he's all wet? Not yours truly. And Paul was fair-skinned. He may pass in Harlem. But he also passes at the country club here."

So David owned the cuckoo in his nest and Angele's tit-for-tat apparently went unnoticed. No one had acknowledged that Jackie had been raped and, after the initial uproar, no one seemed to care who the father of her bastard was. But, so far as Edith ever heard, neither was it acknowledged that Angele's second child had not been fathered by David Thorne. If she had wanted him to be publicly humiliated, she had failed. Then the Lights had moved to California. Maybe if Jimmy Light had been around as Paul grew up, people would have made the connection. As it was, no one ever had. Not even Edith. Not until I came back from New York with my story.

"But what I think now," Edith said, laying down

her knitting so she could look me square in the eye, "is that David really did know. Makes sense. I mean he'd have to've been really sodden not to. He was sodden, but he wasn't dead. And he got even. Planted his own cuckoo in Jimmy Light's nest. That's what I think happened."

I tried to sort it out. It was complicated. David Thorne had three children: Sid Gross, Genevieve Thorne, and Ralph Light. Genevieve had three half brothers: Sid, Ralph Light, and her acknowledged brother, Paul Thorne.

"I wonder how Ralph Light found out," I said. "I mean, he was brought up in California."

"Came across a diary? An old love letter? Who knows. What I'd like to know's this." Edith jabbed her needle at me. "What's that Ralph Light got up his sleeve? Why is it he wanted you to know?"

I said, "I guess maybe that's what we should figure out next?"

"I guess maybe so!"

But it was a few twenty-four hours before I took up the threads Ralph Light had woven into the tapestry. Another pattern was to emerge first.

Chapter 13

I spent what was left of the day thinking over where we were and what we should do next. I'd been on the case exactly eight days, and while I'd learned a lot about the people, I had no more idea who killed the Thornes than the police.

They seemed to be treating the murders as two separate and unrelated cases. At least that's how the newspapers had reported it. David, whose body after all had been discovered in a summer camp, was presented at first as someone on vacation from the big city, another unfortunate victim of the tide of violence rising up from Gotham and overtaking Maine. There were many references to a similar case a few years previously, a murder, still unsolved, of a tourist, in the woods not far from where David was found.

Angele's murder was treated differently from the start. Her Maine roots were uncovered in the first story on her death. Because there was no sign of a break-in, the newspapers suggested that a Good Samaritan act on her part was responsible, that some drug-crazed panhandler had murdered her and then run away. A single bowl of soup, untouched, on the kitchen table, was offered as evidence to support this theory. When, two days after Angele's death, the connection between Angele and David was established, there was an article in the paper about coincidence.

But to me it seemed too much of a coincidence, David and Angele killed within ten days of each other and in much the same manner. Maybe if they had been in the city when they died — but not on the Island. As it turned out, there was a connection; but it had nothing to do with the way they had been murdered.

If the murders were connected and deliberate, however, rather than accidental results of random violence, I couldn't imagine who might have committed them. Certainly not the enigmatic and beautiful Ralph Light with his gold Medusa curls and Michelangelo grace, with a father who wasn't his father, and a message he wanted me to decipher. I had to agree with Edith that in all probability David Thorne was Ralph Light's biological father. Maybe that was all Ralph wanted me to know. But why would he want me to know that? One thing seemed sure to me, Ralph Light had not murdered David Thorne. Let alone Angele. He had gone to too much trouble to let me know of his involvement with the family. I couldn't believe he would have done that if he had been guilty of murdering them.

Another thing I felt I needed was a better understanding of David Thorne. The man eulogized at the AA Memorial I went to — it seemed a year or so ago, not just last week — was well loved and much respected. The speakers had spoken from their hearts and they had said that he was kind and generous and wise.

There's a special honesty about recovering alcoholics. I figured early on it comes from a conscious decision each of us has had to make, a decision to want to live. Our only survival tool is honesty. For con artists, which alcoholics are, honesty is quite a challenge. So at meetings, cons are ruthlessly exposed from the "poor me's" to "I did it for his own good's." "Stinkin thinkin" someone will say, or "Pity Party!"

So, if they said David T. was kind and generous and wise, it wouldn't be a case simply of *de mortuis nil nisi bonum.* Besides, they had laughed, with affection, about his flaws, his faults of character. The picture I'd gotten of the man was of someone who tended to take himself too seriously, who had trouble remembering that the world hadn't been made just for him. Someone who had started, a few twenty-four hours ago, sullen, cynical and close to total despair. Despair, apparently, had remained for him a recurrent problem, although as he had grown in the program he was afflicted by it less and less. At those times he felt he would never get it right, his life, the program.

He had, he said, trouble with his moral inventory. It was a step he had over many years refused to take. He inventoried himself daily, he would say, and there was no point in going back to his childhood to try to get it all absolutely straight.

I didn't do too well on those steps myself — fearlessly taking my moral inventory, listing those I had harmed, and making amends as if by doing so I wouldn't injure anyone — and I had nothing like David T's demons to torment me. Someone, explaining, tears in her eyes, that God had finished his work on David, said David must finally have taken those steps and achieved a kind of perfection, not perhaps as we understood perfection, but as our Higher Power did.

When I knocked on Edith's screen door next morning I asked whether she had called Mrs. Du Lac, worried that I hadn't called her myself.

"About half an hour ago. She didn't mention you. You know, there wasn't much love lost between those two, Angele and she. Not for a while. I don't know they even spoke to each other."

"That's not so," I asserted, "Angele was visiting her mother when David was killed."

Edith looked puzzled. "That's right. You told me that. Well, I guess maybe there'd been some kind of reconciliation. Anyway, Gram was upset. Only child after all. She did say Paul was with her. Brought her the ashes. 'I don't know what to do with them,' she said. Thinks you should bury bodies, not burn 'em."

Wanting reassurance, I asked, "And she didn't say anything about me?"

"Nope. Not a word."

Edith subsided into silence. I began to reflect on

Gram Du Lac and the ambiguous relationship she had had with her daughter, Angele, an ambiguity now extending into the grave itself. At least, I thought, the old lady had her grandson, Paul, with her for comfort.

Edith interrupted my reverie. "Speaking of murder and getting away with it," Edith said. "I also spoke with Jackie Soper this morning. You know, your pal Sid's mother. You said you wanted to talk with her."

"I do, yes," I agreed. There were many things Jackie Soper could tell me, if she would. For starters, did her surly son, my "pal," Sid, know that David Thorne was his father? Did Sid know of the injury his mother had suffered at David's hands all those many years ago? Was Sid aware of how David's indifference had caused the injury of Sid's whole existence?

"Well," Edith said, "Jackie agreed to talk with you. She's not tickled about it, but she'll meet you for lunch. She works at Harrises down to Rockland. The fish packing plant. Hope you're not one of those people who toss their cookies at the drop of a hat. On a day like this . . ." She held her nose. "If I were you, I'd plan to eat my lunch afterwards. Anyway, she's only got half an hour, so you don't want to be late."

Jackie Soper had aged less gracefully than Angele. Several thousand dollars a year less gracefully. Her hair, cinnamon in color, looked to have the texture of straw. She was tall, like Sid, and sinewy, her forearms wrapped in cords of vein and tendon. The floor manager pointed her out to me. "The tall one over there, on the other side. The . . . one, two,

126

three, the fifth table down. See, she's just taking tins now."

"I thought they got off at noon."

"Do usually. There's a big catch came in this morning. Thought it'd be better taking fifteen minutes for lunch. Most of them. Go on over. Won't bother her."

There were a few women sitting on green benches along the wall, eating sandwiches out of paper bags. They had strong stomachs. The place stank of fish. A hundred-foot conveyor belt carried them between two lines of long tables. Two women stood facing one another at each of the tables. Above the belt carrying the sardines, another belt, two feet higher, carried sardine cans.

Jackie Soper had a magician's dexterity. She scooped and filled and pushed packed cans aside with what seemed to be sleight of hand. No one else worked as quickly. No one else hunched over their piles of cans and fish with the same nervous intensity. Others, hands almost as fast, talked to their partners across from them, even laughed some. A few weren't there at all, just their hands. A boy with a cart walked up and down collecting the full racks of packed sardines as they appeared at the end of the tables. Another kept washing down the floor with a hose.

Jackie sensed my presence. She acknowledged me with a kind of nod without breaking the rhythm of her work. She slapped the last tin onto the rack. "Let me wash up. I'll meet you outside at the stairs."

She walked with a stoop, as if she couldn't get

127

away from her table of fish. She was, I knew, four years younger than Angele. She looked ten years older. There was something withered in her. Then I realized she had no upper teeth so that her lips and cheeks were puckered, disappointed looking, as if she were about to cry. She wore a flowered housedress and flip flops.

Out in the sunshine I looked around for a place to sit. "I know you don't have much time," I said placatingly.

"Yeah, but I got an idea." She was surly just like her son. "You want to take me up to Greenville with you." It sounded more like a challenge than a question. I wasn't sure if the challenge was to me or to fate. "But you have to bring me back on Sunday."

"You done for the day?" I hedged.

"I told them."

"Oh." The thought of driving for three hours with Sid's mother dismayed me, but I didn't see a way out. "Well sure. You mean you're coming to Nell's?"

All defensive she snapped, "She invited me."

"Hey, listen. I'm just surprised."

"You mind taking me by my place?" she asked.

At her house she changed into a pair of red shorts and a white tank top. A paper shopping bag was all the luggage she had.

"You been to Greenville?" I asked. In the four years I had lived with Nell I had never seen her there.

She said, "Unh unh." And then she confided, "I been here and up to Bar Harbor." She said it like a native — Bah Hahbah. "Once I was to Augusta."

At her words my funny looking car was

128

transformed. No longer yellow and red. It was white. A white charger, and I a knight who would have taken her to every castle in Spain had I been able. She held her hands clasped tightly in her lap, to contain her excitement maybe.

I didn't see any castles on our way north. She saw a few. Like the Veterans Memorial Bridge in Bangor. "Saw pictures of it," she said, "in the paper."

And Paul Bunyon standing outside the Bangor Auditorium. "He's some tall."

She started talking just outside Dover-Foxcroft. A trickle of words, almost random, at first. Then it started, not gushing exactly, more like spurts of words around intervals of silence, like an unused water tap just turned on. It seems David Thorne had been to visit her a few days before he died.

"He turned up at my table. Just like you. No idea who he was."

Thorne had come at the end of the day and insisted on taking her to the Trade Winds for dinner.

"Only time I been there was one summer waitressing. Before I got on at Harris'. He says, 'Get anything.' Asks do I want lobster. You serious, I ask him. Lobster!" Her laugh was nice, a soft blurred sound at the back of her throat.

"You don't hate him?" I asked.

She didn't answer right away. Then she said, "Did at first. Was only sixteen when Sid was born. Threw me outta school so I never finished. And he was a handful. For me he was."

Nell, it seemed, had found Jackie to be a handful too. When Sid was two she offered to keep him but said Jackie would have to go. "She was movin' to

129

Greenville then. Shoulda done what she said, let her keep Sid. Till I growed up anyways."

Her life for the next ten years or so was sordid. She drifted, snagged for short periods by bars in mill towns along the coast between Ellsworth and Rockland. Sid took care of himself mostly. Some of the guys she brought to bed in the different rooms they called home, rooms above storefronts on the Main Streets of Bucksport, Belfast, Winterport, were good to Sid, took an interest in him, reminded maybe of the little boy they once had been. Took him hunting or ice fishing. But mostly they just asked, "Who's the kid?" if they noticed him at all. Once, she said, someone diddled Sid too. When Sid was ten he up and disappeared, was gone a week or so.

"The first time was summer, so I didn't worry so much. When he come back he was full a tales. Never did say where he went to. I hung around. We was in Belfast at the time. Hung around till he got back. Then we moved on to Rockland.

"I don't remember too clear. But sometime around in there I heard . . . He went missing again. This time it was winter. Anyways I heard how he was up to AMHI, you know, the funny farm. Up to Augusta. I got someone to drive me. They let me see him. But he wasn't glad or nothing. To see me I mean. Can't say as I blame him. Said his father was a prince."

This time I didn't like the sound of her laugh, like metal grinding, harsh as gears stripping. She said, "Thought so once myself. Didn't hit my bottom for a few twenty-four hours after that. Ended up at Kelly Six. You ever been there?"

It's the alcoholic ward at Eastern Maine Medical in Bangor. I hadn't been except to visit. I got dry cold turkey except for meetings. I said, "Once or twice."

"God, I only went the once. Kept me thirty days though. Couldn't seem to get the program through this thick skull of mine. Nell come down and was a family member. How she got started in the program."

She shot a glance at me, shy pride in her eyes. "Sid wound up down there to Surry 'n Edith, she took him in. I'll say this, once I got started in the program my life got a whole lot easier. Not like some I hear tell their story. Edith got me the waitressing job at Tradewinds. Then I got my place at Harris'. Been there ever since, comin' on ten years now."

She was silent through the next two towns, spaced ten miles apart, a good distance for a horse to travel between rest stops. The towns hadn't changed much since the days of horse and buggy. A long tree-shaded Main Street of white frame houses with a general store in the center. Instead of a watering trough, two gas pumps now stood in front, leaded and unleaded.

Outside Corinth she started in again. "I wouldn't've recognized him, you know, it's funny. He was in the program too. Said how he'd been in it goin' on ten years same as me. But he never did do some of the steps — like five — until that year. And he said how what he done to me always weighed like on his conscience. Asked how he could make amends.

"Funny thing was, just him coming like that was amends, all the amends I needed. I'd carried this resentment, like you know, a weight. They'd say 'Let go and let God' and they'd say 'Hand it over.' Like my sponsor'd say 'Give your higher power a chance.' Well I tried, believe me I tried, but it was like something sour inside, like it curdled everything. But just his coming like that. I can't explain."

She lapsed again into silence. I said I thought I understood.

"Funny thing was, he didn't know nothin' about Sid."

"You mean you never told him?" I was incredulous.

Suddenly the old anger flashed. It had a nasty edge, lethal maybe. "Fuckin' bastard. Course not. Figured he needed help more'n me."

She had turned the blade of her anger inward, used it to whittle away her own life and Sid's. Used differently, I thought, it could have destroyed a life completely. For an ugly moment I wondered whether it had. But somehow I couldn't believe she had murdered David Thorne. The serenity I sensed in her seemed unassailable.

Now if David had gone to Jackie earlier to make his amends, who knows? And then I thought, what if there had been someone else David had approached and tried to make amends to, someone like Jackie but without her hard won serenity, someone who had turned their anger fatally against him.

Later, at Nell's, we speculated on this, though the two of them didn't seem to be very interested. They giggled a lot, and I got to feeling like two's company. So after supper I went to my room and read. I was awakened very early next morning by someone at the front door.

"State Police. We're looking for Jackie Soper."

It was Bob Templeton, a local man, young, about thirty. His mother, Alex, was a good friend. His grandmother and Nell ran the little cemetery down the road.

"Hi, Bob. It's me. You lookin' for Jackie Soper? That's Nell's sister, you know."

"Oh, hi Brigid. Didn't know Nell had a sister."

I moved out on the porch of Nell's house with him. "Oh yeah. Jackie lives down in Rockland. She's thinking of moving up, living here with Nell. It's awfully early to be out rounding people up. What's she rob a bank?"

Bob laughed. "No. Worse'n that."

I tried to look alarmed. It wasn't hard. "Say what?"

"No. Just kidding. They want her for questioning. There's been a murder down the coast. You probably read about it. Two murders really. Folks by the name a Thorne. A man and his wife."

"Oh yeah. Read about it. Killed by burglars the police said. Why'd they want to talk with Jackie?"

"Beats me."

I never consciously decided to lie. It just happened.

"Well, they'll be back later today. Like four or so. They went down to Rockland to get some stuff of Jackie's," I said.

He glanced, involuntarily, over to where Nell's car stood parked by mine.

"Took Jackie's car," I said.

"And they plan on bein' back by four?"

"Oh, you know how it is," I improvised. "Like that trip Alex took two years ago. Once you set out down that way, first you stop to see this one, and then the other one."

133

I'd overdone it. He looked alarmed. That trip of his mother's, I recalled, had ended up taking five days.

"Naw. Don't worry. They're just visiting the one place. They'll be back by five. I know because we're going to a meeting over in Guilford tonight. Just, if you call and they're expecting them to show up at ten, ten-thirty, well . . ."

I thought I heard the squeal of oarlocks down by the dock. "Hey, I'd ask you in for coffee but I know you're busy. Want to phone in and stuff." Whatever. Just go away before Nell and Jackie show up with their early morning catch of fish.

He turned and looked toward the east, toward Katadhin shrouded in haze. It was wonderfully fresh and cool still. The morning fog had burned off and the big sky, vast the way it is up north there, was almost violet. The birds were going crazy singing. "Going to be a nice one," he said.

"Hot," I agreed.

I heard the back door open before I saw the tail of his car disappear at the road.

"Nell!" I called. "We gotta problem. Where's Jackie?"

Nell was washing her hands at the sink, her red and black plaid woodsman shirt on the counter. "She got her bass! Swear to God it weighs three pounds. Fought better part of an hour. Know it's Blackie. How many times 's that bugger got away from us? She's down the dock cleaning the rascal. Wanna have some bass for breakfast? I could eat a cow I'm so hungry. Worked up a little appetite —"

"Nell! I said we have a problem."

"So what's the problem?"

134

I told her.

She said, "Why'd you go do a harebrained thing like that? What if he comes back and finds her?"

"I don't know. I just did. That's all. Why would they want to talk with her anyway? Maybe there was something in the will. Maybe . . ."

Maybe, maybe, maybe. The trouble was we knew so little. The trouble was, next to a drifter, Jackie and her son, Sid, were perfect candidates to take a murder rap. No one to protest. Nothing but a public defense lawyer assigned to take their case. A headline to ease public fears. No one to miss either one of them. They lived such expendable lives.

Nell and I cooked up a plan to take Jackie to Canada with me. Quick.

I called Ed before we left, to see whether he knew anything. It was a big mistake.

Chapter 14

Ed was up, minor miracle, and pretty sober still. "You know anything about that Soper woman, Brigid?" he asked soon as he knew it was me.

"Yeah," I hedged.

"Police're looking for her. It's out on all the wire services. Edith thought she might be with you. They want her for murdering David Thorne. Angele as well. They picked up Sid. If you know where that Soper woman is, tell me. This is no murder fifty years old, Brigid. That Soper woman is dangerous. You are in over your head, girl."

"Ed," I said, sounding my best girlish sincere, "thanks for warning me. If she tries to get in touch with Nell, I'll let you know."

Nell had her ear by mine hoping to hear the conversation. As I hung up she said, "What's he say?" I told her, leaving out the part about Sid, afraid she and Jackie both would be off to rescue him.

"Let's move, Nell. Get her bag of stuff. Get her."

Jackman's about ten miles from the border, ten miles of no man's land, deserted, forested, hilly. Ten miles to get real nervous in. A tractor trailer passed us in one short passing space, honked at us. More than our nerves could take and Nell started to question his parentage, then changed her expletive to, "Son of a gun. It's Anna. You know. She comes to meetings sometimes, passing through."

Both my passengers were silent. I think Jackie was stunned with terror. She'd been behind bars before, for soliciting, for OUI, charges that entailed degrading treatment and humiliation. She seemed already to have fallen back into that slough she had spent ten years climbing out of. Her despair was catching.

"Not to worry," Nell said finally. "It's early. Not even nine. They're sure she's headed to the coast. Right?"

"Except for my calling Ed."

She was silent for a bit and when she spoke the gloom had settled on her again. "No flies on that bastard. Friggin' son of a bitch. What'd you go 'n call him for, Brigid?"

"I thought he'd know what the story was, working on the paper and all."

"Gossipin' old busy body's all he is."

It was about then we came in sight of the U.S. border station. There was a line of cars, six or seven. Nell said, "What the hell! They never stop you this side. Only coming back." Then we realized what it meant.

"Shit!" I hit the brakes.

"What the hell you doin'?"

"Getting outta here."

"Don't be an asshole. Hand her to 'em on a silver platter's what that'd be. How far you think you'd get they see you turn around like that? You just keep right on going."

She was right. "So what should I do? Put her into the trunk?"

"First place they'll look. I got an idea. Just keep on, but go kinda slow and keep as far to the right as you can, don't let anyone get between you and Anna," she said.

As soon as we stopped, Nell jumped out. "I'm goin' to kinda wave gaily at you in a minute, me or Anna. You get Jackie out this side and get to hell up there quick when I do."

Jackie was pale with fright. "Put this on," I told her. It was an old baseball cap I use summers driving with the window down. "Turn it around," I suggested, "with the bill in back. Changes the way you look more," I said.

"Hey, Brigid!" Nell bellowed, loud enough to hear on the Quebec side. "It *is* Anna. Come say hello."

"Let's go, Jackie. It's going to be okay." I linked my arm through hers. "Hey, you look terrific. Even Nell wouldn't recognize you." It was true. She looked like a ghost.

At the cab, Nell kind of moved forward on the seat and I handed Jackie up behind her. "You slide in there," she pulled the curtain of the bunk aside. "They never look."

"Jackie," Anna said, her voice quiet and soothing. "You see those blankets? Whyn't you just pull them over you. If they look back there, it'll just be a glance and if they see the blankets mussed they'll just think I took me a snooze."

We'd moved up a space. A car behind me honked. "I'd better get back," I said. "You comin' through with me?"

Anna spoke with authority. "This is what we'll do. When I get to the gate, Nell'l get out and kinda go back and forth between us, not a care in the world. You could get out too, come over. Whatever, don't act impatient. Get in their way even like you wouldn't mind stayin' all day if they wanted. Okay?"

It worked. They knew Anna and joked with her.

"What're you lookin' for this time — dope?" she asked laughing.

"No. A murderer. So don't you go givin' nobody a ride."

"Would I do that? The company don't allow it." They all laughed. Hah. Hah. They knew Anna wouldn't pass up a dog looking tired by the side of the road.

They didn't waste much time with us either. Though they did look in the trunk just as Nell said they would. When we got all through, she was wildly excited, ready to join the CIA. "Wow! Aren't we something!" she said.

It made me sour. "Yeah. But what if Anna hadn't come along," I snarled. "What then."

"She did though. And besides, we wouldn't a needed to wait for long. I know more truckers goin' through Jackman than you could shake a stick at."

She did too. "And what now?" I said, still surly. "When do we get Jackie back?"

"McDonalds. You know. In the first town there."

Our interrogation on the Quebec side of the border was perfunctory. Name, where you from, how long you expect to be in Canada.

In St. Georges, Anna asked if we were going in the business.

"What business?" asked Nell.

Jackie and Anna just giggled. I was amazed at Jackie's recovery, and grateful to Anna for it. On the road again, just the three of us, Jackie said, "You know, yesterday when I met you, Brigid, I'd only ever been as far as Augusta, just that once. Now look at me in a foreign country and nobody speaking English or anything."

We got to Quebec City a little before noon, enough before to get a parking place in that first lot just inside the wall. Jackie had caught sight of the Chateau Frontenac in the distance and asked about it. I told her it was a chateau and that we were headed for it. She was walking on air.

It was cool in Quebec, pleasant. Young people mostly, with backpacks, roamed the streets looking for cheap lodging, for one of the hostels. Jackie was like a child at Christmas delighted beyond speech with the exotic look of things, all the flower boxes and the funny painted signs, the people behind glass, right at eye level, eating croissants and drinking coffee, the women in white aprons addressing the steps of their tiny hotels with brooms.

140

We had to pull her into the lobby of the Chateau Frontenac. She went all shy at the sight of the shiny plastic people breezing in and out. She whispered, "It's just like the movies!" Perspicacious. "Yeah," I said, "It is, isn't it."

Nell propelled her back toward the shops where for a thousand dollars you could buy a life-size porcelain Dalmatian. That's a thousand Canadian, of course. And I called Claire Du Lac.

She was as bracing as a dry martini, very dry and with a twist of lemon. But not so much fun. "I thought maybe I heard the last of you."

I said, "I'm very sorry about Angele." A true statement, but it provoked no response. After a while I said, "I'm down at the Chateau Frontenac." I knew if she didn't say something pretty soon I was going to start to babble. I said, "Would you prefer me to tell you about my week on the phone or to come by?"

"Come," she said. "At three." And she hung up.

We took the funicular down to the oldest section by the river and had our lunch there. Later we checked into the Hotel Terrasse. At quarter to three I started out to Gram Du Lac's. Her niece greeted me at the door, in black, solemn, well trained. Too bad.

"I expected to hear from your sooner," Du Lac said.

I was sitting by my favorite anemone. That afternoon the sun lit the raindrop and made it shine. Jesus looked bored again. All auguries positive, I felt relaxed. Maybe it was just seeing Jackie getting such a kick out of everything. Nell was taking her to buy "something decent" to wear to dinner tonight. In one of the fancy restaurants where they cook French. I just sat there waiting, relaxed and smiling. After a while Du Lac said, "It didn't go so well at the convent. I expected you to call."

I countered the criticism by changing the subject. "Edith Wardwell has the outline and first chapter, rough draft of course, of the history. She likes it. And if you want me to call mid-week, just tell me."

"What happened when you went to see Genevieve?"

"It sounds like you know."

"I called when I didn't hear from you. I spoke to Sr. Barnabas. She said you behaved badly."

"Ah. I didn't meet her."

She said you upset Genevieve. That you struck her."

"Did she really?"

"Well, that you raised your hand to strike her. Sr. Pat stopped you."

"I find that hard to believe."

"I find it hard to believe myself." But it wasn't her own integrity that caused her doubt; it was mine.

I said, "Well, that's not what happened. Did you talk with Genevieve?"

"Yes, I did. But not about that."

"Why not?"

For the first time since I'd met her, Claire Du Lac seemed not quite sure of herself. She asked, "Would you like some tea?"

"Thank you, no."

She wore a large square cut sapphire, a mannish looking stone, on her right ring finger. She had begun to turn it slowly around. "You don't seem a violent woman to me," she said.

"I don't think I am."

142

"What is your story? What do you say happened?"

I told her briefly. Then I added. "Sr. Pat said you've tried to take Genevieve out of the convent. I wondered why."

"Well!" she exclaimed, her uncertainty melting in the heat of her indignation. "Wouldn't you? The poor girl, how many times has she called her grandmamma, 'Gram, please take me away from here!' But when I go for her, they make her say it isn't so. She never called they say. She is happy. Happy there! Of course I want to take her out! That woman!" She shook the sapphire at me.

"Genevieve called you? She asked you to take her away?"

My incredulity exasperated her. Gram snapped back, "You call me a liar?"

"Mrs. Du Lac, no. Of course not. But it's strange, because she did seem content and I really do believe Sr. Pat thinks she is happy being there."

The sapphire started pumping in my direction again. "That woman!"

I said, "She knows you dislike her. Why is that?"

The uncertainty returned. "You do not want tea?"

"No. Thank you, though."

"Some things are very hard for a mother to say."

In the ensuing silence I heard church bells toll and children's voices from the park. The sapphire was getting a workout again, round and round it went circling her finger. She sighed, and then she plunged into speech as if, beneath the icy surface of her words she might encounter her salvation. Or, the death perhaps of some last hope.

"She corrupted my Angele. Such a sweet baby she was. So good. So innocent. I know she means trouble

143

that one, first time I lay eyes on her. That red hair, those hard diamond eyes. Irish trash. Right away, 'Pajama party, Mrs. Du Lac. Please, please. Pajama party!' Well, I caught her."

She relapsed into some somber memory, a reality more familiar I thought than the one we shared at that moment in her parlor. "How old were they?" I asked.

"Angele was ten. That other one was older."

"Oh? How old was Pat?"

"The age of reason!"

"Do you mean she was twelve?"

"She was!" The words rang out triumphant as a capital sentence, the victory, inevitable, of death over life.

"Mrs. Du Lac, I know this is very painful, but what were they doing?"

"My Angele she does nothing. The other one! Hugging and kissing. 'We're only wrestling, Mrs. Du Lac.' Only wrestling. I ask you. Don't think I let her get away with anything. I get her right out of the house. You better believe I do. March that little hussy right home, now."

"You took her home in the middle of the night?"

"Certainly I do. And I keep a close eye on my Angele after that. I sure do. Me and Father Vachon. And it seems all right. We think it seems all right."

But her inner eye, roving the familiar territory, had passed from the triumph to the defeat, from vanquishing the twelve-year-old child to a trouble, whatever it was, heavy enough to bow her with it weight, corrosive enough to eat away the foundations of her soul. She sagged in her chair.

"That David," she said at last, the bitterness

distilled over a lifetime and concentrated. She was adept at blaming others for her troubles, her ability to hate well developed by exercise. I wondered what she blamed David for. I doubted she would be much concerned about the damage he had done to Jackie or to Sid. Her horizons were crowded with grievances more personal. She would probably dismiss Jackie with a shrug and a "she brought it on herself, no better than she ought to be, that one."

I waited.

"Drove her to drink," she said at last. "And then what! He just sits back and looks on? What kind of a man is that? Lets his wife be the town drunk!"

This time her sigh, rising from the depths of her being, carried the taint of sulphur. "Then I wash my hands!" Of Pilate.

"That's all?" I asked, incredulous. "Her drinking?"

She covered her face. The room was filled with a yellowish light from the late afternoon sun. The sapphire winked at me.

"She corrupted the children," she whispered.

The words were almost inaudible. She may not have meant to say them aloud. And at first I wasn't sure I had even heard them. But the words when they registered bowled me over.

Chapter 15

She raised her head and said, "Gen took my typewriter to that convent and I want it back. You get it and bring it to me Saturday."

She had overcome whatever had caused her uncertainty. I was glad. I liked her crusty egocenteredness.

"What about Genevieve. Should I bring her too?" It was *lèse majesté* and I knew it, but the words were out before I had a chance to check them. She looked as if a bad smell had come to her attention.

"You are, I believe the word is impertinent." She put the accent on the last syllable.

"You said Angele had corrupted her children . . ."

"I never did," she asserted. Which told me two things: that is what she had said, and she wished she hadn't. So it must be true. It was a lot to think about. Before I left she insisted on paying me, for travel and a thousand for my "investigations." I took it. Jackie Soper would be going to a very fancy restaurant for dinner that night.

Nell and Jackie had, in Nell's words, gone whole hog. The new dress was linen, or as close to it as you get these days. It looked like linen. White and tailored, sleeveless with wide lapels and a deep neckline, it suited Jackie's lean, hard frame.

"And we got this shawl to wear evenings," said Nell proudly, twirling a gossamer triangle that looked like heather.

In the small hotel room, Jackie modelled with a lack of self-consciousness that surprised me. Her stoop had gone. Without it, she stood about five-foot-ten. In her new open-toed sandals she came pretty close to being six feet tall. Even her head had been transformed, the hair still cinnamon but softly waved, her skin no rougher than the women with yachts in Northeast Harbor. She enjoyed my astonishment. She came up to where I sat on the bed and moved the backs of her hands close to my eyes for inspection, to see the nails long and coral-colored. Two gold hoops hung from her ear lobes.

"We're going to the chateau for dinner," she said shyly.

I said, "Yeah."

To Nell I said, "I don't have anything to wear, not to the Frontenac."

She threw a bag at me. "Those should fit," she said.

The bag contained a pair of khaki pants, a light blue broadcloth shirt, a pair of underpants and socks. The pants and shirt had been marked down. I looked from them to Jackie's reflection in the mirror. "They're neat and clean," said Nell defensively.

"What about my shoes?" I asked.

"Who looks at shoes?"

Jackie got to laughing at dinner. At the menu. It was frog legs set her off. "Good Gawd!" she said. "Frog legs! You eat them suckers when there just ain't nothin' else. I mean nothin' else." She chose chicken cordon bleu.

Next day I left Nell the change from Gram's thousand dollars and hit the road back to Maine. "We may just take us a train ride to British Columbia," Nell said. "But don't you worry. We'll go to meetings wherever we are."

We decided, the three of us, that it would be better if I really didn't know where they were. Nell promised to call Edith every other evening between six and seven, pretending to be her sister. The two of them, Jackie and Nell, were excited, like two kids ready to start on some great adventure, a ride maybe down the Mississippi on a raft. I was jealous.

I arrived at H.O.P.E. in the later afternoon. Edith seemed glad to see me. She hissed, "What is happening! I'm ready to bust from curiosity. And by the way, Ed's been burning the wires between here and Blue Hill trying to get hold of you. I suspect he's been up to no good."

I explained in some detail how no good he had been. "He told me they picked up Sid."

She frowned. "Yes. They did. And if I find out Ed had anything to do with it . . ."

"Did they set bail? What's the story?"

"Not till this morning they didn't. Then they went and put it at ten thousand dollars. Barney — you haven't met Sr. Barnabas yet have you? — well, she went down and gave them what to. They saw the light. You almost always do when Barney shows it to you. Anyway, they released him. On his own recognizance. In my charge! He has to report to me every day."

I was relieved, had been thinking on my way down from Quebec about the redeeming effects a linen suit might have on Sid. That and a car. "How'd he take it?"

"Better than I thought. But something's up with him. You say David never knew about Sid, not until he got in touch with Jackie a few weeks ago. My question's this: Did David ever go visit Sid? Did Sid know that David Thorne was his father?"

"I'm not sure. What Jackie told me is that David promised to set things straight with her and Sid."

"What does that mean?"

"According to Jackie he gave her five hundred dollars on the spot and said he'd set up a trust fund for her so she'd get an income of twelve thousand a year. And that's a good fifty percent more than she ever made at Harris'."

"It doesn't hardly seem like a motive for murder."

"Course it isn't."

"But then," Edith mused, "if she started flashing money around . . ."

149

"She did go looking for a car. She mentioned that."

"And it would just be her word, I guess. David making his amends and all. Her not hating him. Do you know if David got around to setting up that trust before he was killed?"

"Uhn uhn. I don't. But I sure hope so." My mind filled with images of Jackie in a trailer of her own, there on Nell's land, fishing, laughing that blurred laugh of hers.

"Who'd know?"

"Ed?"

"Yeah. Maybe. You should go see him. With a list of questions. Like about Sid, did David go see him or not."

"Why don't you just ask Sid?"

"I will," she promised.

"You know, Edith . . . If David went around looking up people he injured, it could be a pretty long list of suspects. Did you ever think of that?"

She looked glum. She said, "It did cross my mind."

We listened in silence to Willy Nelson for a while. Edith sighed. "What about Ralph Light?"

I said, "Yeah. What about him?"

"He's our one lead outside this small circle here in Maine."

"That's true. Let me ask you something. You think if we find out who killed David, we'll know who killed Angele? You think it's the same person?"

She looked surprised. "Don't you?"

"I guess so. Yeah. But . . . you think it'd be easier to find David's murderer. See, I'm not so sure about that. Also, I'm not sure . . . What I mean is, I don't want Jackie — or Sid either — railroaded. But I'm not sure: One, the only way to prevent that is by solving the murder. And, two, I'm inclined to agree with Ed. I feel like I'm in over my head."

She looked somber and sat awhile, silent. "I know what you mean. I guess I think Angele was killed because David was. I mean, the motive's there. So, yes, it is easier to start with David. As far as being in over your head, at least yours is clear. You aren't trying to get off the hook, or make a deadline, or find an easy out. I've got a nasty feeling that if someone doesn't come up with the right answer, Jackie and Sid will have to pay. So, I'd say let's give it our best shot. It's all we can do."

I nodded. She was right, but I was scared. Scared of the responsibility, I think.

"Let's just keep stirring it," she said. "Something'll turn up. Mark my words."

The next day I met the famous Sister Barnabas.

It was still foggy at 7:30 a.m. when I bounced up the rutted track to the convent. The water-laden air softened the scene. I thought I could discern Sr. Pat's green lawns. I thought I saw the cloisters dimly. Pat opened the door for me. A candle lit the Lectionary, red and gold like Paul Thorne's, lying on the table.

"Come in," she said softly. "We were just having morning service."

"Oh, I don't —"

She put a finger to her lips and with her hand holding mine, she led me firmly to a place at the table. Meekly I followed. Gen wasn't there, but another nun was. Sr. Barnabas I imagined. She was in her fifties, a little older perhaps than I, her face square with her coif and lined, the regular features blunt, almost harsh looking. She gave me a calculating look, figuring, I thought, what she could sell me and for how much. Outside I kept myself all nice and solemn, learned the trick in grammar school. Sr. Pat continued with the Gospel. It was the one about Lazarus. Lazarus the beggar, not Martha's brother raised from the dead.

When it was over, Pat offered me breakfast, oatmeal and fresh milk. "No cheese?" I asked. She laughed.

Barnabas was putting away the wine cup and the candle. "Did you like the cheese?" Her voice was high and thin, unlike the heavy, determined look of her.

"Yes, I did as a matter of fact."

While we ate I asked questions. I asked how long they'd been here and if Gen had been with them from the beginning. She had. I asked about Gen's mental health. I said Gram thought she was unhappy. Barney was defensive, but Pat was oddly silent. I changed the subject. But I kept on stirring. Edith's advice.

"Did your Order buy this place for you?" I directed the question to Pat, but Barney answered.

"Gen's father made it possible. He donated the land and he co-signed for the initial loan," she explained.

"Oh, because of Gen?" I asked.

Pat abruptly stood up, gathering empty dishes, and walked over to the sink. Neither of them answered. It was a puzzling silence, broken finally by the water pump squealing a protest, sounding angry. Pat called out above the noise, "Barney's an excellent fundraiser. That's all. People find it hard to say no to her."

"I am not a fundraiser!" Barney's denial was spirited. "I have never, ever asked anyone for money."

"I'm going to the barn to feed," Pat said. She stood close beside me again. "I'll be back in fifteen minutes."

I turned back to Barney. The pucker of resentment at the corner of her mouth looked sour. "How did you get the money?" Her answer surprised me. She said "God brings it to me." Talk about a conversation stopper. I looked over to St. Joseph: wouldn't have been amazed if he had winked, he looked so consummately patient.

Randomly I made a comment, perhaps it was the baby Jesus who inspired me. "It must be hard having Gen here."

With some heat, Barney in detail corroborated this. She was, Barney said, shiftless, selfish and unreliable. It came, in her opinion, from being spoiled rotten. And Pat hadn't helped matters any. For instance that very morning. Did I know, she asked, how many times in the past week Gen had missed morning service. She didn't wait to see whether I knew the answer. Nuns, in my experience, seldom did.

Pat knew, however. She made another of her mysterious appearances and was suddenly standing there by my side saying, "She missed this morning,

Barney, because she was up late last night. And the last time she missed was five days ago. She had the flu."

"Flu! Mass wine's more like what it was she had."

"Barney!"

"Ooops!" she said. "Did I speak out of turn?" It would have curdled milk, the scorn in her voice.

"Yes, I think maybe you did."

My stirring seemed to have turned up a hornets' nest. I was afraid I might be the next one stung. "Hey," I said, "I think I better run."

"Stay for coffee," Pat said. She had her hand on my shoulder holding me down. "Barney's got paperwork she has to do this morning. We can have a cup of coffee. I'll take one up to Gen."

The battle of wills between the two women was fought with their eyes. Pat's hard diamonds won. Barney rose and, blackly dignified, proceeded out the door. Pat continued to stand with her hand on my shoulder. Savoring her victory? Who knows. I savored her presence.

"Do you like expresso?" she asked.

"I do yes."

"Paul brought us some Bustello from New York."

When it was brewed, she poured three cups. "I'll just take this up to Gen," she said. "I'll only be a minute. I think she'd like to see you." She looked inquiringly at me. "Do you have an hour?"

She climbed the stairs, which were not much better than a ladder, to the second floor. A few minutes later her legs reemerged, then her body, the coffee cup still in her hand. The face she turned toward me was somber.

"She's gone," she said. "Gen's not there."

I asked the dumbest question. I said, "Is her typewriter there?"

"Her typewriter?" Pat, totally preoccupied, put the mug of coffee on the table beside me.

I said, "Could she be out for a walk?"

Pat turned and looked in my direction, our eyes meeting, but making no contact. She was someplace else; whatever she saw there disturbed her. I let a minute pass and then I snapped my fingers. I'd never snapped my fingers at a nun before. It was fun. Slowly she returned to the dimension we shared. "Did you ask me something?"

"Yes. I said she must be out walking and I asked if her typewriter was up there. Gram asked me to bring it to her."

"Her typewriter!" she said with a spurt of anger. Then she sighed, "Oh forget it! I'll bring it down."

She started back up the ladder. I followed. At the top, a long hall, lighted by four dormer windows, stretched to the other end of the building. The wall, roughly boarded, was punctuated every six feet or so by a door. The second one was open. The cell contained a narrow built-in bed and a small desk where Pat stood manhandling a portable typewriter into its case. The light was dim, there was no window, and for several seconds I saw nothing except Pat and the impression of an unmade bed. I mistook the blood at first for one of those dark bandannas the nuns at H.O.P.E wear on their heads. The blood was fresh and lay in sticky puddles, shiny little islands on the mound of her pillow. I let out a cry, something between a scream and a moan. Pat whirled on me, her anger hot now, born of fear, and perhaps frustration.

"What in the hell are you doing here?"

"That's blood," I said.

She turned and looked where my finger pointed as if maybe she hadn't noticed, or maybe she was checking out some wild story she knew was a lie.

"I know." She turned, closed the typewriter case and thrust it at me. "Here's your typewriter."

I took it, opened my mouth to say something, but all my words seemed to have gone on holiday. I retreated downstairs, Pat following me.

It was a while before either of us said anything. I had met Gen only the once and the visit had gone badly. But the impression of her that remained with me, the one that lived in my memory and would in time obliterate the rest, was of a woman so sweet and good that like St. Francis it seemed she could feed wild beasts from her hand and commune with all God's creatures.

Pat said, "Drink your coffee. It's getting cold."

I did, obediently, but it had lost its flavor. I asked, "Are you going to call the police?"

She swiveled around on the bench to face me. She closed her hand around my wrist. She locked my eyes into the hard blue brilliance of her own. "Brigid," she said, "I want you to trust me."

I would follow her into hell, that I could will and so that I could do. But trust her? I laughed.

"It isn't funny, Brigid. I need you to trust me."

"Trust you about what?" I asked.

"Oh. I don't think we should call the police."

An unexpected surge of anger warmed my cheeks. I felt the pulse of it momentarily, heard it beat in my ears. "For Christ's sake, her father's been killed, her mother's been killed, she's missing and blood all over the place and all you have to say is 'Trust me, Brigid?' Are you crazy?"

She captured my wrist again but my eyes eluded hers. "Brigid, it's happened before."

"Oh yeah? That's some remarkable! Dad killed, Mom killed, she disappears. It's happened before, hunh! Who gets resurrected first? Her or her folks!"

"Brigid, Brigid. Shhh." Her fingers caressed my arm. "Of course you're upset. God knows. I remember how I felt the first time."

"What in the hell are you talking about?" But my anger was dying, murdered by the gentle strokes of her hand.

"Gen has taken off before."

"You think she just left?" I was incredulous. "Where'd the blood come from?"

"I don't know. The first time it wasn't blood. It was ketchup."

"That's blood up there on her pillow."

"Yes. It is. The second time, it was menstrual blood."

I thought about it. "That wasn't menstrual blood."

"No. I don't think so either."

"Well! What is it?"

She looked terrible, deeply troubled, deciding between evils I could not even imagine. "The third time . . . It's happened three times . . . The third time . . ." The pause was long as she gathered

157

strength from somewhere, perhaps from me. Her hand lay motionless now on mine. "The third time . . ."

She couldn't seem to get past it. I said, brisk and jarring, "The third time what?"

"She got the blood from a neighbor."

"From a neighbor?" A collage of vampires and crosses in a foggy Carpathian twilight filled my mind.

Through her hand lying on my wrist I felt Pat's shudder. Her fingers trembled the way an aspen trembles in the wind before a storm. "Yes," she said. "A cup of it. Pig's blood. They'd slaughtered. One of ours in fact. Sweetpea."

We each pursued our own thoughts for a while. Hers were ahead of me; I tried to catch up.

That Gen was deeply disturbed I knew already, and after what Gram let slip, I had some idea why. The story of Gen's disappearances was so bizarre I understood Pat's reluctance to call the police. They were sure to commit her when they found her. If they found her. It had begun to seem possible someone intended to wipe out the whole Thorne family. Gen's previous escapades might be no more than coincidence. And maybe, if it was she who had engineered this last bloodletting and disappearance, commitment might not be such a bad idea.

As if she had been waiting for me to get to that point, Pat said, "I'm sure she's all right. And commitment would destroy her. She's very fragile."

"How can you be sure she's okay?"

"She left a note. Like before."

Pat pulled a piece of foolscap from her pocket. The blood had dried. The letters might have been formed by a brown felt-tip marker, an old one with a ragged edge.

The letters were all caps. I KILLED THE SILLY BITCH.

I said, "You find this reassuring?"

"It's the same as the others."

"Can I see?"

"I threw them out. Burned them. Brigid, for heaven's sake! Would I make up a story like this?" Would she? Maybe. To protect her lawns and her cloisters. Maybe. But there was no point in arguing with her so I agreed; I told her no. I said, "When she went away before, how long was she gone? How did you get her back?"

My question was one she didn't want to think about. Worry gathered like a storm cloud between the fine lines of her brow. "The first time, she just appeared, walking through the pasture singing, in time for lunch. She wore a chain of asters. It was September."

An image of mad Ophelia invaded my mind. "The other times?" I prodded.

It was other times Pat wanted to avoid. "Well, the second time she was gone overnight. She just appeared for breakfast the next day."

"How does she get in and out?"

"The hall upstairs ends in French doors that let out onto the roof of that room." The pointed beyond Joseph and Jesus. "I think she lets herself out that way. The ladder was there the morning she came back."

"Does she say anything? Didn't you question her?"

"I did, yes. She seems not to know what I'm talking about. I thought it was better not to press her."

It seemed insane, letting a very disturbed amnesiac young woman run around like that, doing nothing to stop her. "What about the third time?" I asked.

Pat's sigh seemed to empty hope from the inmost recesses of her soul. "Friends called. She'd been gone two days by then. I was frantic, we both were, with worry. They said they'd seen Gen, in Lewiston, at a bar."

The bars in Lewiston there across from the mills down on Water Street are rough. I'd been there once or twice.

"I left immediately to find her. And I did, luckily. She was in Augusta, the outskirts, hitching home. I was so relieved to see her and I was afraid to start right in questioning her. As soon as she was in the car with me she just sort of smiled and fell asleep. When she woke up, back here, it was like before. She just acted like nothing had happened. Just laughed and said we shouldn't tease her when we pressed her at all. And it seemed genuine. I believed her, that she didn't know what we were talking about. That she really believed she had been here all the time."

After a while I said, "What I hear you saying is that it's gotten worse each time."

Pat nodded. Another terrible thought struck me. "Did she . . . Was she gone when . . ."

I didn't need to finish the question. Pat's face told me the answer: Gen had been gone from the convent the night her father was murdered. But Pat's words denied what her face had said. "Don't get funny ideas," she said. "Gen was here." She faltered, "When . . . when those other things happened."

"Oh good," I reassured her, as if I always believed

words over faces. "But tell me this." I went on to a new nightmare. "What I'm worried about is, does anyone else know? I mean could anyone have used their knowledge of the other times Gen disappeared to stage that scene upstairs?"

She looked pensive and slowly shook her head. "No. No one. Just Barney and me."

"Don't you think her brother Paul might know?"

Doubt for an instant dimmed the luster of her eyes. "No way," she said. She shared that characteristic with Gram Du Lac, denying with vigor what she knew to be true. I took "no way" to indicate very possible. Maybe even probable. My next two questions Pat couldn't help me with: Would Paul Thorne be into wiping out his family? Or would Ralph Light? I was pretty sure any information Paul Thorne had would be Ralph Light's for the asking. For a giddy moment I thought of taking Pat with me to New York. We could bring a jar of martinis down to Hudson Street pier to watch the sun set. Our reward after a hot day investigating murder.

This time it was she who brought me back to reality with a question. A question and more pressure on my wrist which still lay caged in her hand. "Brigid, will you trust me in this?"

Our eyes met and I felt hers open to me. I said, "Of course," of course. And then Barney came in.

"Where is she, Pat?" Her voice like the lines in her face was harsh. She held in her hand a coif soiled with mud and something redder than earth: drying blood.

"Where did you find that?" Pat's voice, fear-dried, cracked.

161

"By the stream."

Ophelia wandered again through my mind. "Is she gone?" Barney insisted.

Pat got to her feet. She took the coif and without saying a word to Barney or to me, she left.

Barney brushed her hands briskly, brushing off Genevieve, brushing off Sr. Pat. She turned to face me, brushing still. If she was brushing me off, I was glad to go. But she said, "Stay there. I want to talk to you." Obediently I sank back on the bench.

From the sink she called over her shoulder, "You used to live in Bangor. I have friends who knew you then." The words were innocent enough. It must have been the delivery that caused my stomach to flinch as if my heart had hit it.

"Who?" I asked.

"You don't know them," she assured me, drying her hands on a paper towel.

"Then how do they know me?"

She drew up a chair and settled herself in it, plumping herself, smoothing the black folds of her habit, a broody hen, single-minded, mean and narrow. "The papers," she said.

I'd made the *Bangor Daily* only once and then I was misquoted. I spoke at the first Maine Gay/Lesbian Symposium. The following Monday I was thrown out of my apartment.

To Barney I said, "Oh yeah?"

She had pulled a notebook from some black fold of her habit. She said, "We are desperately in need of a culvert for our road. It washes out every spring. To have it all done properly, a culvert, grading, and gravel will cost two thousand dollars. We don't need the whole sum at once. We can pay in four

162

installments of five hundred. Our credit, thanks be to God, is good. And it's tax deductible."

I just said oh yeah again and waited.

Her notebook disappeared into her habit and she sat there looking at me in a way she may have imagined was benign. I found it difficult to turn my eyes away and difficult to say nothing. I realized my shoulders had drawn together in tension and I was sitting hunched just as I had so many times before while Mother Superior admonished me for being late, for running in the halls, for being slatternly in my appearance. I pulled myself erect and began to breathe deep measured breaths. On the second one my eyes floated free of Barney's.

Unperturbed she went back to using words to bully me. "I spoke with Mrs. Du Lac last week. She must have great confidence in your abilities, she is paying you a great deal."

I let it pass. My head felt swell, the way it does after the first sweet sip of a dry martini. I wish I could remember to breathe deep always. I had an image of myself floating through life like a helium balloon, fat and jolly. I must have smiled. Barney's next words had a cutting edge.

"Mrs. Du Lac has a neurotic aversion to homosexuals." She said it homo-sex-you-als, each syllable in quarantine. "Homophobic I think is the word you use."

If I hadn't already lost an apartment and a job, I don't know what I would have done. Signed on the dotted line probably. Five hundred a month, four easy tax-free installments. Why not. And it's true, she had never once asked me for it!

I skipped a breath and a dark thundercloud of

anger threatened my giddy insouciance. I took an extra deep one and waited for my internal sky to clear. I said, "Oh yeah?"

Still smiling, the good sister said, "After talking with my friends, I believe I really should call Mrs. Du Lac and tell her what they said."

I nodded. "Makes sense. Hey, I'm glad I finally met you. It's been real different! By the way, where's the stream? I want to say goodbye to Pat."

On my way back to the barn, I began to tease the possibilities from this new information.

It seemed to me that Barney must have blackmailed David Thorne for the convent and the land. By then, I knew enough about David to be pretty sure that once he got around to making amends for his own misdeeds, he was likely to prescribe the method as good medicine for everyone else. Barney would certainly regard that kind of advice as a veiled threat. I knew Barney was a blackmailer. Would she murder too?

The sound of weeping guided me to Pat's side.

Chapter 16

It was a meandering little stream. Where Pat sat, under an apple tree shedding blossoms on the ground and on her hair, the stream was trying to make an ox bow, the jut of land almost an island. Pat sobbed over a bundle of black cradled like an infant in her arms. I knelt beside her putting my arm across her shoulders. The bundle was a nun's habit. The ground around us had been mauled, the turf dug up as if a struggle had taken place. In a while her sobs subsided, but neither of us moved.

"Is that her habit?" I asked at last.

She nodded.

"Do you still think she's all right?"

"No." It sounded like wind soughing through the lost high branches of a pine tree.

The stream made silvery sounds as it went about its sapping and robins, vandalizing the earth, enchanted the air with their song. "Pat, hadn't we better call the police?"

"No. No. You don't understand. There's nothing they can do. She, she's . . . I can't explain. She won't come back. But, please, Brigid. You said you would trust me. This has nothing to do with, you know, her father. Not with his murder."

I drove up to Ed's place shortly after noon. I found him clamming on the mud flats in front of his house.

The tide was out and the odor of the sea — iodine, salt and decay — blew strong in the wind. With his pants rolled up and a clam hod on the mud beside him, he was bent over digging, singing *Kevin Barry*. His tenor, I thought, wasn't what it used to be. Or perhaps my brain needed a few drinks to fine tune it. A jar of what looked like martinis lay propped against a rock, two little cocktail onions floated disconnected and lonely in a liquid that was clear and innocent seeming.

"Brigid! Where on earth have you been? I have a bone to pick with you, girl." He clambered up out of the mud to my side. "First, join me in a drink. 'Tis the first day of summer, Brigid. According to Ed Kelly! I have opened the gin. Remember, Brigid, the good old days — before you turned so God Almighty sour — our first bottle of gin when summer came."

166

I hope I never forget. I never could drink gin.

"Yeah, Ed. I remember."

"So, join me for old time's sake."

"Later. Tell me about the bone first."

He opened the jar and took a slug of gin. One onion disappeared. The other looked disconsolate floating alone quite close now to the bottom.

Sitting next to me there on the rock, he stunk — of gin, of mud, and decay. It was perhaps the stink of corruption. He was at that point in his day's drinking when the world and all of its creatures seem wonderful and I was glad. His chiding would be done in good humor.

"You lied to me," he said.

"You went and called the State Police," I countered.

"Only a precautionary measure. How did you get her into Canada?"

"Who says I did?"

He looked at me scornfully.

"Okay. She got across in a truck. Up where they sleep."

He thought about it a while. "Where is she now?"

"Who knows."

"You mean to tell me, Brigid, you don't know where she is!"

"Yep. Nell and I thought it would be better if I didn't. That way, if you tortured me she'd still be safe."

He shook his head, more in sorrow than in anger. "Brigid, Brigid. I don't know what's come over you." He eyed his martini jar, then postponing gratification, he said, "And that do-gooding old busy-body, Edith

Wardwell. She got Sid out of jail. She and Barney."
He changed his mind and drained the rest of the gin.
"We'll go in the house in a minute, and I'll mix us a
couple of gins with tonic water. I have a lime. We'll
do it right."

"What do you have against Sid?" I asked. "And
Jackie. They seem like victims to me, Ed. Blaming
victims doesn't seem your style. What's it all about?"

"Ah, Brigid. That's it, is it? Your old Donna
Quixote routine. When are we ever going to break
you of it? Stay for supper, I'll steam these clams and
I'll toss a salad."

"Sure," I said, but without hope or illusion. There
had been too many invitations like it. They ended
with Ed asleep and dinner still in its component
parts, laid out on kitchen counters, unprepared. It
didn't bother me. I used to do the same.

In the house I declined "my" drink. It made him
grumpy. "Well, here's mud in your eye then, Brigid."
He took a healthy swig and let out a contented sigh.
If I didn't get him talking soon, I could forget it. At
the rate he was downing gin it would soon be too
late to get anything out of him but snores.

"Tell me about it, Ed. I don't believe Sid's smart
enough to get away with murder. Jackie either. They
seem to me more like patsies. I bet you anything you
like — how about a drink? — that someone's framed
them. You prove to me that Sid and Jackie are guilty
and I'll drink to it."

What the hell. If Sid and Jackie were really guilty,
I'd need a drink. I'd need more than one. "I'll take
my bottle of Jamisons," I said.

"But it's summer, Brigid! We're drinking gin and
tonic."

He should have been a disarmament negotiator for the Pentagon. "Whatever, Ed. You name the poison. But tell me first."

"Ah, it's sad. I'll be the first to admit it. Poor fellow. He never had a chance. I know that. But . . ." He shook his head, the sorrow of the world in it, swimming, drowning.

"Tell me, Ed."

"Yes. Well . . ." He had begun to cry, the tears seeping under his lashes. He jabbed at them with his thumb as if he could push them back inside his head again. "You see, he told Angele. Dear sweet girl. You've got to stop them, Brigid."

I didn't know who the dear sweet girl was, Angele or me. And I wasn't too sure who "he" was. It was probably too late to make any sense of what Ed would tell me. I could try. "Told her what, Ed?"

He looked up surprised, angry suddenly. "Don't you listen? Are you deaf? He told her Sid was coming. She begged him . . ." The tears began again.

"Is this the night David died?" I prodded.

He nodded, the tears flowing freely now, his hands occupied with making another drink. "The same."

"But Angele was in Quebec."

"That was later." He drank as if he were thirsty. Then, wrathful, he said, "Mr. High-and-mighty setting the world to right. Mud in your eye, Brigid. You should let Mr. Thorne-in-your-side be a lesson to you."

I was glad for the anger. It was more becoming than his maudlin sorrow. I said, "Are you saying that David saw Sid the night he was murdered, that David was going to set things right with him?"

"Are you stupid? Must I say everything twice

169

over? Are you hard of hearing? For God's sake have a drink! A terrible man. Terrible. Always was, right from the beginning. Poor Angele." His eyes once more welled with tears. "He raped her. You didn't know that, did you."

"Angele?"

"Don't be a focking eedjit! Gen! Gen! Genevieve! Oh ho! You didn't know that did you. Think you know so goddam much."

I was appalled, unbelieving, and yet I began to wonder. I said, "Ed, are you telling me that Sid raped Gen? When?"

But he was too far gone: with gin, with indignation, with zeal for justice or revenge. He only repeated his charges. "Sid is a dangerous man, Brigid. You've got to stop him. Enough of this running around tiltin' at windmills." Then he said, "Tell you something else you don't know. Angele'd had enough. Enough of your Mr. Crown-a-Thornes. We had set a date, Brigid. Yes, a date."

"What do you mean you'd set a date?" The thought that Ed had gone around the bend was reassuring in the circumstance. "Angele was married, remember?

"Never heard of a Dominican vacation?" He leered. "Well, she was goin' to go on one. Got 'er the tickets myself. Only one little problem. Mr Thorne-'n-thistle wouldn't let 'er go. I told 'er I had plenty. Told 'er I'd tart up the little ladies. Turn 'em into condos. We could live anywhere. Ireland. Dingle. Palm trees and no bugs I told her. Paradise." He lapsed into a puzzled silence, trying perhaps to figure what had gone wrong with the dream, his paradise lost.

I asked, "How could David have stopped her?"

He expelled his breath in an explosive burst. "Mr. Know-it-all. 'No money,' he says. 'For your own good,' he says. Needed to spend all his money on his own dirty conscience! Oh Brigid. I don't want to die an old drunk." He began to sob. "We would have sobered up. Angele and me. On our own. Over there. In Ireland where we belong. Who was he to tell us what to do?"

I said, "She stayed with him because of money?"

His anger flared again. "Don't go being judgmental yourself, Brigid. You're a lot like him you know. The two of you." He minced his face and words. "Oh, no thank you. I don't drink. Shouldn't yourself, Ed. Bad for your liver. Worse for your soul. I'll take care of my own bloody soul, thank you all the same. Sanctimonious bastards, the lot of you!"

After a pause, his voice rose again, wheedling this time. "You don't know, Brigid, what it is to be poor, what it does to you. You mustn't think badly of her. Poor little girl. She was so afraid."

"Afraid?" I asked. I remembered the fear I had seen in her eyes. And I remembered the name that had evoked it: Sid.

It had gotten to be late. It was after six. The sun outside the window shone brightly, unaware it seemed of our murky lives. Unaware or uninterested. The murky part of me wanted to defy the sun's indifference and stay there with Ed to share with him the oblivion he had found.

I rose to leave.

"Your drink, Brigid. You owe me a drink. And we haven't had our clams yet."

"Ed, I owe you one. Next time."

171

I left over his protests. They seemed indifferent too. The sound of gin splashing reminded me of Pat's little stream sapping away at the bank where she sat. It seemed a long time ago.

Chapter 17

I knew when I left I should go to dinner and I should go to a meeting. But I did neither. I went to Edith's.

Fact is, I was looking for a fight, though I didn't know it, perhaps because the person I wanted to have it out with was myself. Ed's accusations against Sid had shaken me. He had been too drunk to lie. The part of me loyal to Jackie, to Nell and to Edith was up in arms against the part that had listened to Ed and believed him. A drink would do wonders to patch up the differences I had with myself. And a drink was a price both parts of me seemed willing to pay to achieve some kind of peace.

If I was looking for a reason to get drunk that night, I couldn't have picked a better person than Edith to visit. It turned out she too was spoiling for a fight. I should have known she was in pain, her arthritis bad, the minute I walked in the door. Maybe I did know. Maybe I didn't care. Maybe it suited my purposes.

Her greeting was perfunctory. My hello may have been surly, but she only nodded. "Where's Sid?" I asked.

"Who wants to know?" she said.

"Gen's missing."

"So?"

"So? That's all you have to say is 'so'?"

"Yeah. So. What's that got to do with Sid?"

"Did you know he raped her? Did you know —"

"Hey! Back up. What are you talking about?"

"You didn't know," I said cockily, satisfied I had caught her attention, that we could proceed with this conversation on my terms. Maybe I reminded her of her dad on the TV behind me, grinning at her over my shoulder.

But my illusion of control was brief. She snarled, "And neither do you. You about to accuse him of murdering his father too?" She sniffed the air, her face sour, Cary Nation smelling gin. "Oh that's it! Spent the afternoon with Ed again, have you."

She didn't accuse me of drinking, not quite. If she had, I could have denied it. But the accusation lay there between us, unspoken, and it gave her moral advantage. It also distracted me. I yearned to clear

174

my name, restore my honor. Ed was an old reprobate, but not Brigid Donovan. It undermined my attack on Sid just as it was meant to. Lamely, I said, "David was expecting a visit from Sid the night he was killed. I think someone should talk to him. Don't you?"

"I think," she said, "I've had enough of this conversation."

So had I. I stormed out and headed to Greenville.

I wasn't in the house ten minutes when the phone rang. I let it ring. I didn't need any more grief that day. But it wouldn't stop. Finally I picked it up. It was Bob Templeton.

"Brigid? I have instructions to pick you up and question you," he said, then added deferentially, "I'm awfully sorry."

"Could we talk in the morning, Bob? I'm bushed."

"Sure. No problem. It was the INS at the border who identified Nell going over with us. He has your names. You gave them to him. Brigid, you told me she'd gone to Rockland and would be back that evening. Saturday. I could bring you in as an accessory." I could hear his deference slipping. "I'd rather not, of course," he patched the hole.

"Tomorrow?" I suggested. "Could we talk tomorrow? Say eight?"

"Good. Thanks, Brigid. And, Brigid. I really am sorry."

This time I said, "No problem."

My decision to drive to Canada that night was reflexive. I was too tired to think. I had a justification of sorts: to deliver Gram's typewriter to her before I was incarcerated. In reality I felt too wild to sit still let alone go to bed. Cold. Sober. I had to hit the road for somewhere. The typewriter provided an excuse.

I spent the night in Lewis, across the river from Quebec City. Next morning at the house on Parc des Gouverneurs, Gram's niece opened the door. Her English was only marginally better than my French, which meant we were in trouble. Our conversation looked like a game of charades. I was given to understand that Gram was napping. I thought for a silly moment that the niece was telling me she was dead. I handed over the typewriter. Inspired by some thought, she motioned me to wait. She came back in a moment with a ball point pen and a pad of note paper. She gestured for me to write. I did: Mrs. Du Lac, here is your typewriter.

I paused. I decided it was foolish to mention that Gen was missing; it could do nothing but cause her to worry. I signed my name. The niece said "Merci" and "au revoir" and so did I.

It was a little after two and for the first time in days it seemed, I didn't have something urgent to do. Nothing urgent except to get to a meeting. There was one at 7:30 in Jackman. I could make it easily. But I decided to play it safe and return to the States by way of Vermont. I made a meeting in St. Johnsbury. It wasn't half bad.

Chapter 18

I decided to stop by the convent on my way to H.O.P.E. to make my amends to Edith. I felt light-hearted. It must have been the wind buoying my spirits, but it felt like a conviction that Gen was safe, back home again, a conviction based I hoped on some deep psychic knowledge.

No one answered the door, so I wandered back to the barn. Pat was there mucking out the hen house. She thrust the pitchfork into the matted straw and dressing. She leaned on it, her body bending toward mine, her eyes looking at me thoughtfully. It was intimate in there, close and warm, the air cloying, sweet with decay like a rumpled bed that's been slept in too long or been made love in too much. She said, "Gram Du Lac's trying to reach you."

The light was dim, too dim to see the sparkle in her diamond eyes, just the hardness of them. "Is something wrong?" I asked.

She said, "Whatever gives you that idea?"

The sarcasm jarred me; it seemed unlike her. For a while we just stood there in the gloom. She said, "Anyway, she said to call her."

"Okay. I guess then Gen's not back?" I couldn't read her expression, the light was too bad. "Do you have a minute? Could we talk?"

She thrust the handle of the pitchfork at me. "You ever muck out a hen house before?"

I hadn't. I said, "Sure."

"Well, finish up here. When you're done come by the house. We'll have lunch."

Lunch was goat cheese again, with chives. I asked about Barney.

"She's out."

There was more to Pat's abruptness than sorrow and worry. But I couldn't imagine why she would be mad at me. We ate a while in silence.

I began to tell her about Barney's attempt at blackmail. I hadn't meant to. I only opened my mouth to fill the silence separating us. My story didn't seem to surprise her.

"So did you pay her?" Pat sounded uninterested. Disinterested maybe. I wanted her to be indignant, and I wanted her to be on my side.

"No I didn't! That's blackmail." I had another thought. "Pat, did Barney blackmail David?"

178

"I don't know."

I waited a while before I said, "Would she call Mrs. Du Lac and tell her?"

"About you? Probably."

Was it glee I heard below the surface of her words, or was that just my paranoia? "You said Gram called me; when was that? Did she leave a message?"

"Yes. She called just before you got here. She said you were to call this number in New York. Ask for Jonathan. I wrote it up on the wall." She looked at me for the first time since we sat down to lunch. The despair in her eyes was as deep as space and as coldly empty.

I blurted, "What did I do?"

"I suppose," she said, "you don't know who Jonathan is."

"Pat, I never heard of Jonathan. Do you know who he is?"

She brushed the question away. She said, "Did you go to Quebec yesterday?"

"Yeah."

A nasty thought had left its trace in her eyes. She said, "She seemed . . . smug. Like she knew about Gen."

"That would make her smug? I think it might frighten her."

"What did you talk about?"

I felt my temper begin to slip. "I didn't see her."

"You went all the way to Quebec City and didn't see her? Do you expect me to believe that?"

"I really don't care whether you believe it or not. Actually," I said thoughtfully, trying to explain to myself that mad midnight dash to Quebec City to

179

deliver a typewriter, to avoid being questioned by the State Police, "Actually I think I just wanted to find Jackie, Jackie Soper, Sid's mother."

"I didn't know he had a mother," she said. It seemed to make sense for a minute and then we both started to laugh.

"Well," I said, "he does. And his father was David Thorne."

That seemed to come as no surprise to her. I told her about going to Rockland to talk with Jackie and of our escape into Canada last Saturday. I told her about my talk with Ed and the circumstantial evidence against Sid. I said, "Did you know Gen had been raped?"

Pat looked stricken but not surprised.

"Well, when I found that out, I thought I should find Sid." Then I told her about the fight with Edith, the midnight call from Bob Templeton, and my flight to Quebec.

"Poor Brigid," she said. "Can I get you some coffee?"

"Have you seen Sid?" I asked.

"No. But then we don't much. Why?"

"Why? I told you. He was apparently the last person to see David alive. And we know he's violent."

"Sid?"

"Yes. Sid. I told you he raped Gen. You didn't seem surprised. I took it that you knew."

"Not Sid."

My temper, flammable as kerosene, caught fire. Fist pressed to lips I managed, barely, to block a hot retort. When I could say it softly, I said "Who then?"

She lowered her head pushing her thumbs against the bony ridge of her eye sockets, against the sinus cavities there, trying maybe to push away pain. She teetered a while on the edge of a decision. I held my breath not wanting to blow her in the wrong direction. Finally she shook her head slowly and said, "I don't know."

Our sighs met in the middle of the table. I said, "Pat, it must have occurred to you. No, let me start that again. It seems to me that someone is making a clean sweep of the Thorne family." I counted them off on my fingers, going real slow. "David, Angele, Gen. There's only Paul left. Ed Kelly is certain it's Sid. David did approach Sid to make amends, and Ed knows that Sid visited David the night he was killed. Ed thinks Sid's gone berserk."

She said nothing, but I sensed the resistance in her. I prodded. "Well? What do you think?"

"I don't think Sid is violent," she said.

I looked at the ceiling. Reluctantly I admitted, "Another thought has occurred to me. Do you know Ralph Light? Have you heard of him?"

"Paul's friend from New York?"

"Yes. So you do know him."

"Not really. But when Paul was here after Angele died, he called him. Quite often in fact." A fleeting smile lit her face for an instant.

I told her about my encounter with Ralph Light, my near encounter with his father, and Edith's theory about the twisted relationship that formed between the Lights and Thornes in those summers long ago.

The silence following my story was amiable enough, but then Pat said, "So you're willing to substitute this Ralph Light for Sid Soper? As your candidate for mass murderer?"

"You find it amusing?" I asked, huffy.

She touched my arm. "No, Brigid. I don't. I'm sorry. I'm just tense and I have a terrible headache. I don't think anyone has abducted Gen."

I said, "So you don't think she's in any danger."

"No. I didn't say that. I said I don't think she was abducted. I do think she's in danger."

Pat had returned to the edge of the old decision and was teetering again. This time she came down on the other side. It was quite a story she had to tell. No wonder her head hurt. So did mine when she came to the end of it.

She began with an account of her banishment in the middle of the night from the Du Lac household when she was only twelve. It had been a searing experience and had left a scar.

I said, "Mrs. Du Lac seemed to think you were seducing her daughter."

"Actually it was Angele trying to seduce me."

"Pat! She was only ten."

"I know."

When Gram had told me the story, I thought she was outrageous. But I believed Pat. Maybe because, even after all these years, she was trying to discern her responsibility in what had happened. Gram, with no discernment at all, simply pinned the blame on someone else for what went wrong, in her life and in the lives of all those she held dear.

Pat and Angele had continued their friendship at school and through intermittent letters after they became adults. Pat was Genevieve's godmother, this despite the protests of old Mrs. Du Lac. But she hadn't seen much of Gen and for this dereliction of

182

her vows, Pat held herself responsible for much of what had happened.

When Gen was seventeen, she came to New Hampshire to be with Pat, to finish high school in the convent; she hoped to enter the order. Angele had begged Pat to take her; Angele was afraid Gen was on the verge of a breakdown.

"I hadn't seen Gen in several years. She surprised me. I remembered a charming little girl, full of mischief, a tomboy. She was so fragile. Well, you've met her. She seemed so, so purified. So delicate I was afraid to touch her, spiritually or in any way.

"Then one day we were working in the garden. It was spring. She'd been there about six months. One of the cats brought us a mouse. It was still alive and the cat began to play with it, torture it really, the way cats do. I didn't pay any attention, I was bent over digging. Then I heard a strange laugh. It was like a chuckle, sly, a really ugly sound. I looked up and there was Gen watching the cat terrifying that poor mouse, and she was grinning. She was enjoying it. No question. I was totally horrified. I threw a clump of dirt at the cat to chase it away, to give the mouse a chance to escape. Gen said, I couldn't believe my ears, she said, 'Fuck you! Leave the cat alone.'

"I was stunned. Then I said — she's only seventeen, remember — I said, 'Gen! What kind of language is that. Don't ever use that word to me again.' And she looked at me and she said, 'What language, Aunt Pat. I didn't say anything.' I was literally speechless. Then I told her to go water the transplants or something and she did as if nothing had happened. That night after prayers I took her to task for her language and she said, 'Aunt Pat, don't tease me. I don't say things like that.' I talked it over with my Formation Director. She said to keep my eye on her. And I did. Remember, Angele had told me she was worried about her mental balance.

"It kept on happening, periodically. Once I saw her picking off a butterfly's wings. Another time a duckling, too young to swim, was drowning in its water, and she just stood there watching it with that absorbed look on her face, a kind of glee. Other people began to notice. And it turned out she had a name for those times. She called herself Jonathan."

"Jonathan!" I said. "That's who I'm supposed to ask for when I call that number in New York."

Pat nodded. "I know. I was confused and suspicious. I don't trust Gram as you know."

"With good reason."

She smiled. "I was afraid you were in cahoots with her. I even thought maybe she was threatening me. Well, to make a long story a little shorter. It was decided that Barney, Gen and I would come to Maine and start a sister house here. Gen couldn't continue where we were. She had upset too many people. Her father by then had been sober quite a few years and he was very helpful. He found us this land and donated it to us. You asked whether Barney blackmailed him. I honestly don't know. But she wouldn't have had to. He was overjoyed to be of help."

For a while we were silent, each absorbed in her own thoughts. Then Pat took up her story again.

"We'd been here a while, a year anyhow, and Gen seemed to be better, calmer. Then, one night she came into my room. Woke me. We still didn't have

184

electricity, so it was very dark. I don't know what time it was. She said she was cold and she wanted to get in bed with me. Her voice sounded different. Not like Jonathan. It was more like the girl I remembered, or what I would have expected her to become. Though I didn't think about it at the time. I was too sleepy.

"Well, those cots are narrow, but I scrunched up against the wall and she came under the covers with me. And pretty soon she began to talk. She called me Aunt Pat, the way she used to when she was small. It was a terrible story. But she told it matter of factly. I never doubted for a moment that what she said was true.

"Ever since she could remember her mother would take her and Paul to bed with her. In the afternoon for naps or, as they grew older, after supper. She would be drinking of course. And she would fondle them, and have them fondle her. She told them that was love.

"As they grew older, naturally, they realized something was wrong, that other children didn't have this experience. Angele told them it was their secret, and she seldom let them go visit other children. She seldom let other children come visit them either. By the time they started catechism and preparing for First Communion, the conflict and guilt were becoming unbearable. Gen tried to tell. She told her Grandmother who said she was wicked to talk like that. Her father started to cry and to spare him, she never mentioned it again.

"In my bed that first time, she said she just wanted me to know how grateful she was to Barney and me for letting her come to live with us. She fell

185

asleep finally and the next day she seemed happy. But she never mentioned our talk. And she had that same purified fragility.

"It wasn't long after that, Gram arrived unannounced on our doorstep demanding that Gen come home with her. Gen wept and begged us not to send her away. I sent the old lady packing. But I knew we had trouble. Gram stormed out of here accusing me of corrupting her daughter and her granddaughter and threatening that she would tell the world.

"By this time I knew that Gen suffered from what they call MPD. Multiple Personality Disorder. You know. Sybil. Faces of Eve."

I didn't really, but I nodded.

"Separate personalities develop. I mean totally different people coexist in the same body. I didn't find out where Jonathan came in right away. The girl, Gen, I mean to distinguish her from the nun, came to my bed again in the middle of the night."

Pat buried her face in her hands for a while as if the memory was more than she could bear. What she said next filtered through her fingers, muffled and hard to catch.

"When Gen was eight, David took them, her and Paul, on a camping trip. It was something he did every summer. Paul left early that year to go to summer camp. It was the first time David and Gen had been left alone. The night Paul left, David got to drinking. His maudlin sentimentality gradually changed to something more overtly sexual, and finally to rape. The next morning he didn't even speak to Gen. He sent her home alone and then he disappeared. It was years before Gen saw him again.

186

Of course she blamed herself for his disappearance. When he did finally come back he was sober and he had developed a deep spirituality. A year later Gen asked to join the convent."

Pat felt that Gen had found in her father's new piety a way to bind her own life together. "I've read a lot about this sort of thing," she said. "Often girls who have been sexually abused become promiscuous. And I think it is a miracle that Gen escaped alcoholism, given that both her parents are alcoholic."

I remembered, perhaps unfairly, Barney's charges against Gen concerning the Mass wine. But I let it ride.

Pat said, "I think David, in the way he came to terms with what he had done, gave the children a . . ." She groped for words. "A life preserver. A way to save their souls." She seemed happy with this thought, a sort of silver lining. But to me it seemed a way to ignore the cloud.

Sensing my skepticism, Pat elaborated. "See, everyone else either pretended like nothing was happening, Angele for instance, or that everything was someone else's fault. Like Gram. But David was different. He went around preaching the Serenity Prayer and Twelve Steps. But actually he was holding out hope. And then there was his life. The way he had changed. What the children learned from David was that they could accept reality and live with it. With God's help," she amended. "it was a real antidote to despair."

I said, "What about Jonathan?"

"Jonathan."

She said it like a death sentence. I guess maybe that's how she thought of it.

"I think Jonathan must have appeared after the rape. It happens sometimes. I mean that a separate personality is formed after a trauma like that; and also, for a woman, it often happens that the personality is male and aggressive, someone who's better able to protect himself than the victim. Jonathan was all those things: he was male, aggressive, violent — like with the cat."

I said, "It sounds terrible. But I guess it makes sense."

It did make sense in a bizarre way. I said, "Pat, *is* it so terrible?"

"Do you mean can we put up with Jonathan?"

"Yeah."

"Probably. God knows we've lived here with him for several years. It's more like he can't put up with us any more."

"The disappearances."

"Yes. The disappearances. You see, what I think happened is something like this. As Gen grew stronger by just being here — when I say Gen I mean that wonderful child I used to know — she wanted to grow up. But the nun, that pious, spiritual construction that David inspired, she was too fragile, too rigid. She wasn't able to grow. See, if she changed at all she'd fall right off that little pedestal she's got herself balanced on and she'd shatter. Or at least that's what she's afraid would happen.

"Now, I realize this conflict in Gen isn't quite normal, but it isn't pathological either. I mean, I've seen lots of young girls enter the convent and after six or seven years, when they get to be say twenty-seven or eight, they want out. Sometimes they don't even realize that's what they want; they can't face it. It can be a terrible struggle. You know, between who they really are and who they thought they were, or who they wanted to be. I even saw someone break down under the strain of it. Well, that was the kind of conflict going on in Gen, but worse, because with her the saint had probably kept her from sinking into some awful degradation. I really believe that. Drugs, prostitution. Who knows."

I must have looked skeptical.

"Oh, Brigid! It's true. From alcohol to drugs, from sleeping around to, uh, hooking. It happens. It happens all the time."

I let it go.

"Well, it *is* true." She emitted a bleak laugh., "I've become an expert." She waved at the wall of books. "Among the confessions of saints over there, you'll find some studies of girls, boys too, who've been through the kinds of experiences Gen has. Some worse, if you can believe it. I wonder how many of the saints were abused as children? Augustine? Theresa of Avila? Anyway. What I think happened is that Jonathan began to want to get rid of St. Genevieve."

It took me a while to work out the implications. Pat gave me the time. She said, "The girl struggling to grow up, who confided in her Aunt Pat — and confided successfully; I accepted the dreadful things she told me and didn't reject her — I think that girl called her grandmother and begged to be taken out of the convent. And I think Gen must have mentioned, or she admitted under cross-examination, that she had been in bed talking with me. Gram is very insistent that I've corrupted her."

Pat sighed, then went on. "But when Gram came

189

to get her, she was terrified and the saint refused to go. That's when Jonathan stepped in. The first disappearance of St. Genevieve was accompanied by a very ritualized killing. Ketchup, remember. But each time it's gotten closer to being real."

"Good God, Pat. That's horrible."

"Yes. Horrible. I've tried to talk to her. But it's hard. Of course she won't acknowledge all that stuff going on inside of her."

"Yeah. It's kind of crowded in there." Bad joke, but I had to get a little distance.

"Pat. Is Jonathan violent?"

"Yes."

"Violent enough to kill somebody?"

"I don't know. I'm afraid of him."

"Could he have killed in revenge?"

"You mean David and Angele?"

"Yes."

"I don't know."

"But you think it's possible."

"Possible yes. But I doubt it."

"*Could* he have?"

"Yes." She said it reluctantly. "Gen was gone the night David was killed. I don't know if Jonathan appeared when Angele died, but then it's not clear exactly when that happened. She had been dead a while when they found her."

"But it's possible?"

"Yes. Gen was alone here several hours that evening. And I didn't do a bed check. I thought she was here when we got back. I glanced in her door and it looked like she was in bed. But she could have faked it I suppose. You must realize, Jonathan only

190

appears briefly. A day or two at the most. And I only say that because the last time Gen disappeared she was gone two days. Around here, Jonathan comes for, oh it might only be minutes. I should tell you too, I don't dislike Jonathan."

"But he frightens you."

"Yes," she said, "he does."

The picture was disheartening. For each of us. What it boiled down to was that we both wanted to put Jonathan away. Our problem was like his. He couldn't do away with St. Genevieve without doing away with himself and Gen. We couldn't dispose of him without locking up the two Gens. Gen known and Gen unknown. Saint Gen and, who knows, Gen the harlot maybe.

I said I thought I should go to New York to check it out. "I wonder why he, she, wants to talk with me?"

"I've thought about that, and I don't know. That's one of the reasons I thought you were up to something with Gram."

It was then she asked to come to New York with me.

I said, "No problem." We decided to drive.

Edith seemed glad to see me. "You find Sid?" she asked first thing, not even bothering to say hello.

"Who wants to know?" I said, relieved, and echoing her reply of two nights before.

She laughed. She was feeling better. I was forgiven. For the first time the possibility crossed my mind that Edith might regret her part in our quarrel, been fearful of losing me. "I'm sorry about the other night," I said.

"Oh forget it. What are you up to now?"

"I'm going to New York."

"You staying at your friend's apartment again?"

I nodded. I said, "You willing to call me again at eleven? Not tonight. But tomorrow?"

"If you want me to, sure. I'd be glad to."

"I'd feel more comfortable."

"Will do then. By the way, Gram's trying to reach you. And Ed. So what else is new. Gram has a number she wants you to call. In New York."

"Ask for Jonathan?"

"Eyuh. You got that one already."

"Yeah. What does Ed want?"

"Who knows. He probably wants you to arrest Sid for him."

If I hadn't been so full of myself, so eager to be on the road with Pat, my new partner in crime, it might have registered that Edith was holding out on me. If I hadn't been in such a rush to be with Pat, I might have replied with something like, "But I don't even know where Sid is." I might have remembered that Nell was going to call Edith regularly. If I'd paid attention, I might have realized that Edith would send Sid to Canada to be with his mother and his Aunt Nell.

Instead, I said, "Did you know that Ed and Angele were planning to get married?"

"Says who? Says Ed?"

"You don't believe him?"

Edith snorted. She said, "Are you kidding? Angele

give up all that do-re-mi? No way. If Ed thought that, he was kidding himself."

Silently we pursued our own thoughts. To me it added up to a motive for murder. But I couldn't somehow imagine Ed killing anyone. Especially not Angele. Reluctant as I was to face it, he did love her. Had loved her, old reprobate that he was.

Chapter 19

It was after midnight when we arrived at West Beth. Even so the city was hot and muggy and people were on the prowl. I found a place to park across from D'Agostino's. The man at the desk remembered me and gave up the key to Erika's apartment without a question.

"That place gettin' a workout," he said. But I was too tired to pay attention. Just nodded and offered him a million in devalued currency — thanks.

Upstairs, Pat was charmed by the apartment as I had been. I settled down for the night in the palanquin again, while she slept in the sleeping loft over Erika's desk. I got up a little after six, found the Medaglia d'Oro from the last time. The smell of it brewing brought Pat from her bed. She wears pajamas. So do I.

At 7:30, I called the number Pat got from Gram. It seemed oddly familiar as I dialed it. It was.

"Emmaus," a sleepy male voice answered.

"Sorry," I said. "Wrong number."

Pat looked puzzled. I explained. We decided to go on up unannounced.

Turned out Paul wasn't there and neither was Gen; but Jonathan had been there and he had caused quite a stir. Ralph was summoned to deal with us. He was dressed in tight white shorts, the Magnum look, the outline of his balls, squeezed to the side of his fly, provocative I guess if you're into it. He wasn't so high-waisted, so high-hipped as Tom Selleck, and he walked like a dancer, feet slightly splayed, high-arched and delicate in leather thongs. Except for the shorts, what there was of them, he was naked. His chest, like his head, was covered with tiny gold curls. "Hello, Sister," he said to me with a high intensity smile of recognition.

Pat and I turned down his offer of coffee. Pat told him how urgently she wanted to find Paul.

"Do you know where he is?" she asked.

"Gee, Sister, no I don't," Ralph said, smiling. "Sorry."

He clearly was lying. Or perhaps he only wanted

us to believe he knew, but wouldn't tell, where Paul had gone. Pat blew up. "Look here, young man!" she began.

Ralph, continuing to smirk, raised his hand, checking her flow of words. "I'm getting myself some coffee. Sure you don't want some?"

In his absence, Pat fumed. "That lying bastard! He knows perfectly good and well where Paul is."

I said, "Let's get out of here." And I pulled her, protesting, out onto Lexington with me. "Later," I said. "I'll explain later."

Truth is, I couldn't have explained right then. But I sorted it out during the long hot subway ride to the Village. It was Pat calling Ralph a lying bastard that made me look at the puzzle from a different perspective. David Thorne had had not one but two bastards. In Maine, several people, including Ed Kelly, knew about Sid. But no one had known about Ralph Light till I came back from New York with the news. No one except Angele, that is. Because I was certain David would have let her know when he paid her back for being unfaithful.

If Angele had said something to Ed like 'His bastard's coming to see him,' Ed would have assumed she meant Sid. But she could just as well have meant Ralph Light. And I could better imagine Ralph paying that last visit to David Thorne than poor Sid.

I explained all of this to Pat on Hudson Street pier that evening. We had taken a picnic lunch and watched the sun go down over Jersey. She wanted to go manhandle the truth out of Ralph, but I urged caution.

"You're not afraid of him!" she scorned.

"Nah," I said. But I lied.

196

* * * * *

Pat and I started to get ready for bed about ten.
"What's it like up there?" Pat asked.
"In my palanquin? It's fun. Come up and see."
"How do you get up there?"
The stairs are in a Gaudi-like structure against
the wall, a sort of grotto, the steps simply six niches
that serve as footholds. It had been designed as a
fountain and jardiniere. But all the plants had died
and Neff, the cat, had a pillow where once the pool
of water formed.
"You could break your neck," she observed.
"Yeah. They were young and romantic when they
built it. I love it."
The platform holds a mattress and not much
more, just a headboard piled with books and a bit of
floor space around the sides. Pat sat beside me, her
feet placed primly on the floor. I had drawn the
curtain on my side against the breeze from the
windows. I said, "Close those curtains. It's quite
wonderful in here with all the curtains closed."
She did. She had turned off the lights on her way
to bed. Inside the curtained space, in the dim glow of
the night light, we were two kids in an Arabian
Nights adventure. I said, "Do you have a pin?"
"A pin?" she asked.
"Yeah. We could be blood sisters."
That's when I thought I heard the door open.
She started to say something. I said, "Shhh," and
turned off the night light. She was about to protest,
but then the light came on at the head of the stairs
and she froze.
It was two men. One of them was Ralph Light.

197

"They not here, man. They gone to Maine."

"Yeah, they are."

"You think they ony one Maine car in New York? You crazy, man."

God, what a fool I am, I thought, leaving the car parked practically in front of the building. I wondered how they had gotten in. I remembered then the doorman saying the apartment had had a workout. Maybe Ralph had simply asked for the key as I had and then made a copy of it. He had been familiar with West Beth. Maybe one of the doormen was familiar with him. I wondered what he had wanted the apartment for. I wondered what they wanted with us. I wondered how long it would be before I found out.

The excitement of Arabian Nights in flesh and blood reality has its good side and its bad. Pat's shallow breathing in my ear I liked. But the feeling of my own breath struggling through the paralyzed cavities of my lungs, that I didn't like at all. I tried to do deep breathing silently. But soon the pungent smoke of Gauloise cigarettes drifted up from below and made it difficult to breathe at all.

"It feels creepy in here tonight," the other man said. "What's in that thing up there?"

"Nothing. It's called a palanquin."

"I feel like something's in there."

"Go up and check it out."

I heard him get up and walk over. He stood beneath us. His voice sounded as if he were in there beside us. My breath stopped altogether. So did Pat's.

"Hey. How you get up there?"

"You don't. It's just for decoration. Like I told you."

"It's weird. Whole apartment's weird."

"Yeah. Would you stop pacing."

The phone rang.

It was 11:00. It was Edith. God bless her. It was Edith.

They let it ring. Edith didn't give up easily and after a while the ringing got on my nerves. You could feel the tension rising as the four of us waited, counting the seconds between rings, each ring, insanely, filling me with hope, the silence with dread.

"Whyn't you answer that motha' fucka'?"

"It's for them."

"How you know that? Could be for you."

"Answering machine's not on."

"So?"

"They're expecting a call. Otherwise the answering machine'd be on. Means they're still here. Like I said."

The ringing finally stopped and I experienced despair. Though I knew it was irrational, I felt abandoned.

The conversation between the two downstairs was desultory, but it told us a couple of things. They had used Erika's apartment before to sell drugs; and Ralph's stash had come from David Thorne. He seemed to be using his connection with Emmaus to launder money and he hoped to use Genevieve to circulate drug money in Maine through the convent. He had apparently already spoken with Sr. Barnabas, who seemed to have mistaken him for a messenger from God, coming as he did with so much money.

"She was a pushover," Ralph told his companion. "I asked her whether Emmaus could use the convent's checking account 'cause all the New York banks kite checks. You know how it is, I told her. You get a donation, you're desperate. But you wait a week for the check to clear, and then you pay some bill, and Bingo! They bounce the check anyway and charge you fifteen bucks. Friggin' bank says it didn't have time to clear. What it is, they're not done making money off it. She said she would be glad to help us out. She says —" He started laughing, "She says, " 'It would give us a chance to do God's work.' "

I could imagine that Barney was glad to help out. Talk about kiting! I thought I knew which of them would laugh last over any money Ralph Light might give to Sr. Barnabas, and it wouldn't be Ralph Light. He'd be lucky to see any of it again except as a well-drained road, pigs, and cloisters maybe.

The phone rang again. It was the same as before. Edith hung in there for about thirty rings. It was nerve-wracking, but when it stopped I felt desolate.

"Wha we gonna do when they get here, man?"

"Scare the shit out of them."

"Din you say wan from the convent?"

"Yeah."

"You don' think scarin her bad business maybe?"

Ralph just laughed. The sound was unsettling.

I could imagine Ralph leaning on us, using his big buddy to intimidate us. There wouldn't have been much we could do. It would have been hard to prove anything against him. But now that we had both heard about his drug dealings and the way he had involved other organizations in his operations, it was different. If we alerted Fr. Xavier, the evidence of Ralph's manipulations would be revealed as well, probably, as evidence to tie him into the drugs he was selling. At the very least, he would no longer be able to use the Emmaus accounts as a cover.

And, of course, there was the matter of murder. There was no longer any doubt in my mind that Ralph had killed his father and then, to protect himself, had murdered Angele.

He might plea bargain one crime against another, but the way I saw it, Ralph Light would be doing time. I didn't think he would last long in Attica. Which made me think Pat and I wouldn't last long if he discovered us up in that bed.

Pat's mind must have been running on the same track as my own. Her fingers had completely cut off the blood in my arm. I gently pried them open. The needles of pain as circulation returned were hard to endure silently.

The phone rang again.

"Goddamn fuckin' telephone!" Ralph's buddy shouted.

The telephone stopped mid-ring and then there was a crash. He had pulled the phone from the wall and flung it across the room.

"Asshole! What the fuck are you doing?"

"Fuckin' thin drivin' me crazy, man!"

"You could of unplugged it!"

"Why the fuck din you then?"

"Jesus Christ, you're an animal."

"Thas rye. So shut the fuck up."

About ten minutes later someone knocked on the door.

"What the fuck!"

"Shut up."

Pat was back messing up the circulation in my arm and my breath was having trouble moving my lungs again. We heard the door open.

The encounter below was brief. The intruder was apparently a security guard and she was armed. As it turned out, Ralph's buddy carried a gun, too. But thinking it was just Pat at the door, or me, he hadn't bothered to draw it.

"Who are you and what are you doing here?" the new voice asked. But she didn't seem much interested in Ralph's answer. "What happened to the telephone?"

Ralph said, "I wondered the same thing myself. It was like that when we got here."

I didn't hear her reply. Maybe she didn't bother to make one. She said, "Real slow, I want you to leave the apartment. Don't try to break and run. When we get downstairs, I'll want you to give the doorman some identification. Ms. Duncan may want to press charges."

"Hey, you got this all wrong. We're just friends," Ralph began to protest.

"Then there's nothing to worry about. Is there?"

About ten minutes later came a knock at the door. Pat and I had only begun to unwind from the tension. It was almost one. We had been trapped in the palanquin two hours. It was the security guard.

"Just wanted to see you were okay."

"How'd you know we were here?" I asked.

"A lady from Maine called. She wants you to call her back. You can use the phone in the lobby."

Edith said, "Knew it was past your bedtime. Then the phone went dead. So I called the operator. Told her what'd happened and what I was afraid of. She got me the West Beth number and I talked with the guy at the desk. People say New Yorkers aren't helpful are just plain crazy."

The next morning over coffee, Pat and I decided to go our separate ways. She wanted to stay in New York until she found Gen; I thought I might as well get on back to Maine. It looked like my murder investigation was over. Pat would stay at Emmaus, where the security might not be perfect, but was better than at West Beth.

I said, "You'll tell them about Ralph running his drug money through the Emmaus accounts."

She nodded.

"Who's going to tell Sr. Barnabas?"

Pat got to laughing. I asked, "What's so funny?"

"She's incorrigible. She'll keep all that money, you know. It's no wonder she says God brings it to her." Then she added wistfully, "I wonder if there'll be enough for cloisters. After the road gets fixed."

Talk about incorrigible.

Edith had told me Gram wanted to see me. It was Saturday, the day my report to her was due. I looked forward to telling Mrs. Du Lac the case was solved. That David had been murdered by his illegitimate son, Ralph Light. That Angele, and Angele alone, had known Ralph was the last person to see David the night he was killed. And that Angele too had been murdered by Ralph.

I looked at an atlas and figured I could make Quebec City by evening shooting straight up through New York to the outskirts of Montreal and over. I thought maybe I could round up Nell and Jackie and bring them home with me. By way of Jackman. With Ralph behind bars, why not. I called Edith to expect me for lunch on Monday.

"Hey, woah! Not so fast," Edith said when I finished reciting my optimistic interpretation of events.

"What do you mean, not so fast? I told her. They arrested Ralph Light."

"For murder? Did they arrest him for murder?"

"No. I told her. They arrested him for breaking into the apartment."

"You told me he had a key."

"Yeahbut, they had no right to it."

"Yeahbut, yeahbut. Listen, dollars for doughnuts, they're out already. The both of them."

"Out!"

"Yes. Out. And by the way. Ed, your buddy Ed, is saying he and Angele were married."

"Say what!"

"You heard me. He claims he and Angele were married. Two days before she died. One reason he's going after Sid. David did leave him and Jackie a trust fund. Now Ed's saying where Sid murdered David they can't inherit. Doesn't say who'd get the money, but I have a nasty idea he thinks he'd maybe get it."

My old pal Ed. I was too stunned to reply. Edith said, "You still there? Ma Bell doesn't charge by the word, you know."

I said, "I'd still like to see them. Jackie and Nell."

"Okay. Do that. They'll be there when you check in. Only for God's sake, don't go trying to bring them back. Not yet."

"Where'll they be? At the Chateau de la Terrasse?"

"If that's where you go, that's where they'll be."

I got through the long hours of driving by imagining my reunion with Nell and Jackie Soper, imagining the change a week as a tourist would have made in Jackie. I tried not to dwell on the implications of what Edith had told me, nor on the possibility that she might be right about Ralph's being released. I would rather have the cops after me than Ralph Light. I wondered whether he and Ed would get together. I wondered how much my long friendship with Ed would be worth if I got in his way.

And I thought about Pat, about those bizarre two hours we had spent side by side on the edge of the bed in that palanquin; thought with regret that we would never be so close again. Not in this life. And I decided that whatever money I got from Mrs. Du Lac I would give to her to help build the cloisters. I could sit in them some day, eating goat cheese, listening to St. Genevieve chanting plainsong.

If Sr. Pat could find St. Genevieve, could get to her in time. But even if Pat did find Gen, what would she do with Jonathan, and with that other Gen who didn't want to be a saint?

And I wondered what it was the girl Gen wanted to become, what she wanted to be that Saint Gen would not allow. I imagined Pat would soon find out, and I yearned to be with her when she did. Maybe I could help. Donna Quixote to the rescue once again!

Which led me to reflect that the closest Sunday meeting was in Dover-Foxcroft, thirty-five miles from home.

But then, if Edith was right, and she probably was, we wouldn't be going home. Not soon anyway. Not tomorrow.

That's how I spent the time driving to Quebec City. Nearly twelve hours of chasing myself in circles, trapped inside this hamster cage I call my mind.

Chapter 20

Next day in the parlor of the house on Parc des Gouverneurs, Gram brushed my greeting aside. "I have heard from Genevieve. And you must do something about it." She held a sheaf of papers in her hand. They looked like letters the way they had been folded. She handed them to me.

"There's proof," she said.

Proof of what, I had forgotten. I glanced through them. They went back about three years, all signed Gen or Genevieve, all typed, and typed on the same machine. The "e," missing a piece of its tail, gave each page a distinctive look.

Her tone peremptory, Gram instructed me to look at the last letter, the one she had just received.

"Dear Gram," it started, as did all the others. It seemed to be written by two people. The first two paragraphs, written in a childlike way, were about activities in the convent. The third paragraph was different.

"She made me come to her bed again last night. She makes me let her put her arm around me. She makes me let her kiss me. She talks and talks about Mother and how they loved each other. I can't stand it. You've got to help me. When you came before they made me tell lies. What should I do?"

I studied the signature. Gen. I looked through the other letters more carefully. The signature was the same, a large immature hand, the letters carefully formed and rather square. And several of the letters had that curious change of style which I knew now to reflect the two Gens. None of them, however, contained the charges made in the most recent letter. In the others, the Gen who wanted out had simply said she was unhappy, unhappy with the discipline, unhappy with having to care for the pig, milk the goat, and get up before dawn. But nothing actionable. I looked at the date of the last letter. Wednesday, June 17. Gen had left the convent on Monday.

I asked, "Where was this mailed?"

She was ready for the question.

"Why, in that place where she lives. Surry."

"Do you have the envelope?"

"Of course I don't have the envelope. Why should I keep the envelope?"

Her show of indignation was forced. "No reason," I said.

I didn't want to alarm her; there was no point in telling her Gen was missing. But I was certain her letter was a forgery. It made me mad. She had paid me fifteen hundred dollars to swipe a typewriter so she could set up Pat. The rest of it was a smokescreen. She hadn't wanted me to investigate a murder any more than she had wanted me to write a history of H.O.P.E. She hadn't even wanted me to frame Sid. It was Pat she wanted to frame. For a crime Pat never committed. For a grudge Gram had carried for more than thirty years.

But someone had committed the crime. Ten-year-olds don't try to seduce their playmates as Angele had tried to seduce Pat, not unless they themselves had been seduced by someone older whom they trusted. Seduced or forced. At that age it seemed hardly to matter.

I wondered who it had been, wondered if Gram knew who it was. And I wondered at the life Gram had led of denial, of always blaming the wrong person for the wrong thing.

I said, "I want you to tell me something."

The mouse that roared. My tone must have shocked her. She said meekly, "Yes?"

"You and Angele didn't get along so well. Isn't that right?"

If she had been more cautious, she might have denied the rift. But Gram couldn't resist her resentments. "What was there to get along with?" she asked.

I didn't know. If she meant drunks aren't really there, I couldn't argue. I glanced up at Jesus on the mantel. He didn't know either. He looked sad. I said, "I don't know. I rather liked her."

She looked at me contemptuously, her eyes bright with knowledge. The eyes told me Barney had called her; but it had made no difference. Gram's needs overrode her prejudices and she had needed me: to get her the typewriter to forge that letter from Gen. What else, I wondered, did she have for me to do. Because I knew when she was done with me she would get rid of me, and quickly.

She said, "Many people like Angele." She might just as well have said, "Many people go to hell."

"But you didn't," I persisted.

"I am her mother."

"But you were estranged."

"Estranged. Yes. Like strangers. We were."

"Then why was she visiting you the night her husband was killed?"

"You say very strange things. She visited me. That is all. She is my daughter."

I debated going around that circle again. Instead I asked, "When did she get here?"

The answer again was prompt. "Late afternoon. We have tea. My niece, Marie. She bring us tea."

"How did she get here?"

There was a flicker of hesitation before Gram replied. "She drive."

"She came in her car?"

"Yes."

"Were you expecting her?"

Gram folded her hands in a contented way. "No. She call me. 'Gram,' she say, 'I want to see you.' 'Why?' I ask. She say she love me, she want to see me. I think, 'Why not?' She is my daughter. It is only natural. So I say, 'Of course. Come up.' Then the surprise! She say to me, 'Gram, I am here.' 'Here?' I ask her. 'Yes,' she say, 'Here in Quebec City. I am at the Chateau Frontenac. I come now.' And she come and we have tea."

Gram's expression was beatific. She had surprised me. The details of her story gave it the verisimilitude of truth, and I believed her. I shuffled around in my chair thinking I might as well go. She said to me, "Don't you want some more money?"

I said, "Sure."

On the floor by her chair was a large leather handbag. From its interior she extracted an envelope. She handed it to me. I took it. It felt thick, too thick to stick in the pocket of my jeans. I didn't know where to put it so I held it in my hand.

"Count it," she ordered.

I pulled out the bills. They were twenties. American. There were fifty of them. It took me almost a minute to count them. As I did I became aware of the chirpy voices of children in the park. I heard the niece humming in the hall outside. She was dusting the banisters maybe.

"That's too much money," I said. "You don't owe me that much."

"Yes," she said. "You earn it."

I knew how I had earned it and I didn't like it. But twenty five hundred to deliver the typewriter and Sr. Pat into her hands still seemed steep. Especially since I sensed Gram could drive a hard bargain.

"The murder of my son-in-law still is not solved," she said. "We have an agreement. Until we catch the killer, you work for me. Five hundred a week and expenses. We agree, isn't it?"

211

"Yes."

"Well then."

I worked it out. It sounded like a bribe. A handsome one, from my point of view. Maybe Gram figured it was cheap: to avoid a scandal. And she thought she had my number, or my price. But even if I accepted that logic, she had overpaid me. I had been on the case only three weeks.

"It's still five hundred too much."

She waved her hand. The one with the sapphire. It winked at me, an old friend. "I keep track," she said. "And you work hard. Maybe you don't make it up next weekend."

And maybe I never see you again, and the five hundred is a bonus for the typewriter, I thought to myself.

"What you do now?" she asked.

"I think I'll get some lunch."

She smiled at my pleasantry. "Your friend, Mr. Kelly, he thinks that man Sid is responsible. I think you should follow that."

"Right," I said, and started to get up.

"Before you go," she checked me. "There is the business of my granddaughter. I want you to bring her to me."

I settled back down again. "I can't do that."

"But you must," she assured me. "I send copies of this letter —" She waved the forgery at me, "— to the Mother House of Gen's Order and to the Diocese in Maine. I want Gen out of there when they investigate. I want her here."

I just bet you do, I thought. And I thought after all I had been underpaid. I decided she could twist in the wind with her forgery and her interference. So I

212

said, "Oh, okay. I'll do my best." My best, as I saw it, was to do nothing.

She said, "I expect you with her on Monday."

I replied, but to myself, "You do that, kiddo. Expect away."

I strolled over to Place de Hotel-de-Ville hoping I might find one of my fugitives. When I saw Jackie emerge from a tabac across the Rue Buade, I thought at first it was just another false sighting. She looked terrific. She carried a small paper bag, the kind they use for postcards. She wasn't avoiding me; she just hadn't seen me, and she was looking for someone. Her glad smile told me when she spotted whoever it was. For a silly moment I thought all that brilliance was for me. Then I realized it must be the young man who had just passed by me, jostling me as he went. I crossed the street in his wake. He was tall and young. I couldn't see his face but presumed he was good-looking. He was dressed in slacks and plaid short-sleeved shirt, like a thousand other handsome young men in Quebec City that afternoon.

I wondered where Jackie had met him. She had eyes for no one else, didn't notice me right behind him. When they met she put her hand on his sleeve intimately, possessively. He took the bag from her hand, then pulled her hand through the crook of his elbow. Together they began to stroll along the boulevard. I had witnessed the scene a million times in a million movies. They did it well. The only thing wrong was the difference in their ages. They couldn't do much about that; their gestures though were perfect. It suddenly dawned on me who the young man was. It was Sid. I felt somehow that I shouldn't intrude, so I followed.

213

On the Rue des Jardins they took a table at a sidewalk cafe. Sid ordered for them both. If my mind had not been crowded with other images of him, surly, irascible, irrational, he would have seemed an ordinary young man, politer than most, debonair as Robert Powell. Were my mind not contaminated by the knowledge of Angele's relationship with her two children, I would not have noticed that Jackie and Sid seemed more like lovers in Paris — a Hollywood version — than mother and son on a summer vacation. it was Nell who broke my reverie.

"Well, son of a gun! I thought maybe we'd missed you." She pointed toward her charges. "Cute aren't they."

I said, a little grumpily, "They act more like lovers than a mother and her son."

She giggled. "I know. That's what's so funny. I think it's great. They've neither of 'em ever been anywhere." She groped for words to clarify an idea, as if perhaps to discern it clearly herself. She settled for, "They remind me of someone."

"Yeah," I said, "Cary Grant and Ingrid Bergman."

She looked surprised, happy surprised. "Oh yeah. That movie they always show."

I nodded. A winter favorite on Sunday Matinee. Channel Two out of Bangor. I felt oddly relieved.

Jackie was tickled pink to see me. Her words. Sid just rolled his eyes around in their sockets. The old Sid. Not at all something I had ever seen Cary Grant do. I remembered what Edith told me: Sid thought I was weird.

Sid had joined them, Nell explained, five days before. I told her I had to be getting back. I said I thought in just a few days it would be all right for

214

them to go home too. I told them about the trust fund David had set up for them, that they could, if they wanted to, live in Greenville with Nell. Jackie and Sid held hands and looked happy. Sid said, "I'm going to get me a car." And Jackie said, "I wonder if I could get a trailer with one of them bow windows at the end."

I asked Nell if she'd call Bob Templeton and tell him all that had happened, and ask him whether I could return to Greenville without being thrown in the slammer. When she returned from the phone booth she said, "Bob will meet you at the border. He'll take you into custody there." She acted like that was a good idea.

I asked her what the hell she meant. Sid scowled and told me to watch my mouth.

Nell said, "It's okay. I told him you have the case solved. You do, don't you? You've got that look."

I nodded, glad none of them had been around to hear my other solutions. But Nell was right. I did have "that look." I must have: I had "that feeling." When the pieces finally fit, they lock in place in a way that's unmistakable. And now, for the first time, all the pieces fitted. I knew, and Nell could tell.

She said, "Yeah. I thought so. I told him it's just a question of tying up some loose ends. I said if he wanted us for neighbors he better let you do that. I told him Sid was with us and he knows darned good and well none of us didn't do nothin'. Well, of course, he knew that already. He's just following orders. I told him all his orders amount to is railroading poor folk. He said the law's to protect people, but I told him BS. Pardon my French. He knows. Anyways, he's willing to let you in through Jackman."

215

It made me uneasy. "What if he holds me?"

"Don't worry," she said. "He won't. He has to take you into custody. If you go through Jackman, somebody does. But he won't hold you. And if he does, you just call his mother, Alex. She'll take care of him. I called her and told her. Just to be on the safe side."

It made me nervous; but I didn't have much choice. I needed to see Ed and I needed to check out some things with Edith. I had to find out whether Pat had found Gen. The pot I had begun stirring on Edith's instructions had come to a boil.

I gave Nell all but five of Gram's twenties. Jackie said she was going to pay me back. I said, "Yeah."

Chapter 21

I left Quebec City at four that Saturday afternoon and arrived in Jackman a little before dark. Bob Templeton was at customs waiting for me. If he bore any rancor for my having lied to and eluded him, he didn't show it. I told him what I knew. He didn't seem to find any of it sensational. He didn't even seem surprised. "it happens all the time," he said. "Keeps on happening and happening. Do you know," he asked, "that almost all child molesters were molested? Almost all abusers were abused when they were kids. It's endless." He looked discouraged.

I did know as a matter of fact. But I had a thought that was a little less pessimistic than his. I said, "Even though abusers were abused themselves, that doesn't mean all abused children will grow into adults who abuse. It can stop."

Bob's eyes, looking at me, seemed to be missing something, maybe an illusion he had lost. "Yeah," he said. "So there's hope." I don't think he meant it.

I tested him. "I guess you don't really think Jackie and Sid are guilty?"

"How would I know? Mom says you can depend on Nell. I guess I do. You say Mrs. Du Lac wants you to bring this Genevieve woman to her. How do you plan to do that?"

I shrugged. "Who knows. Actually, I don't think I will. That letter is a forgery. Hey, I should hit the road."

"Call me," he said.

I promised I would.

I timed it nicely with Ed the next morning. He was still in his bathrobe. Irritable, but rational. he offered me a screwdriver. Said it would put the bloom back in my cheeks. "You look tired, Brigid."

I said, "Edith tells me you're a widower."

The way the land curves there at Ed's, the bay is to the west and the deck in the morning is shaded. So it wasn't the harshness of the summer sun being unkind to him. Ed plain looked bad, his face a yellowish color under the stubble of his beard. I wondered whether he was headed toward detox, and whether it would do him any good. He poured himself another drink.

"Ed, you're killing yourself. You look awful."

I saw tears begin to seep from the corners of his

eyes. "They would have railroaded her," he whispered. "Framed and railroaded. She wouldn't have had a chance."

I leaned over and put my hand gently on his shoulder. "What is it, Ed?" I asked.

He looked up at me, startled. "What? Oh, Brigid, it's you. What are you doing here?"

"I'm visiting you. Ed, did you discover David Thorne's body?"

"Oh, Brigid!" he breathed. "That I did. What a pitiful sight he was lying there, and the hammer beside him." Ed looked up at me then, his eyes pleading. "Understand, Brigid, he was a terrible man. A bully. Used his money to manipulate her. Wouldn't give her her freedom. But . . . Oh, my God. It was dreadful seeing him like that. And the worst part, don't you see, was I knew they would blame Angele."

He looked around for his glass. It had fallen from his hand and rolled across the deck. "It's over there," I pointed.

"I need a drink. Let me fix you one, Brigid."

I said maybe later.

As Ed poured gin into his glass and onto his robe, he continued to explain. "I cleaned up. I washed all the plates and the glasses and I put them away. I picked up all the cigarette butts. They were hers. Every last one of them. Not one of them was Sid's. That's what made me angry."

He stared at me belligerently, or perhaps it was fervidly; perhaps it was to convince me. "See, I knew it was Sid killed him. Angele said before she went to David that night that the bastard would be coming by." then he wheedled, "Brigid, you know how sorry I felt for Sid. If he'd left some trace of his presence,

219

it would have been different. I would have understood. I would have helped. But he left that scene to implicate Angele. Angele who had never done him any harm! Ah, had there only been time I would have fetched a cigarette of his brand and left it there. See how he liked that! But there wasn't time. I had to get Angele away. And provide her with an alibi. She would be the first person they'd go after. So I had to make it good.

"I called her mother. The bitch owed her that. She agreed, the old lady. I drove Angele up that night. We decided, Gram and I, to bring you into it, Brigid, in case something went wrong. In case, despite everything, the police went after Angele. You were our insurance policy. I knew Nell was Sid's aunt. Knew we could keep tabs on him through you.

"My only regret is that I didn't call the police and tell them what I knew. It was a pity that stayed my hand, Brigid. And look what happened. He murdered her. It's that I can't forgive him. My poor Angele, my poor dead lamb."

He worked on his pity a while in silence, his pity and his grievance. I worked on what he'd told me.

I didn't buy Ed's self-righteous defense of his treatment of Sid. There hadn't been much he could have done to implicate Sid without risking Angele. Not to mention how he had destroyed evidence and failed to report a murder. Something else was bothering me, though. I said, "Ed, why did you marry Angele so soon afterwards?"

"To protect her." He seemed surprised at my question. "Married her so they couldn't make me testify against her. Her alibi was pure gold. But it didn't matter. The filthy little bastard murdered her

220

too. And I intend to see he pays for it. Don't stand in my way, Brigid."

I tried to tell him about Ralph Light and my intuiting that it was he Angele had meant when she said the bastard would be coming by. An unfortunate choice of words. Ed was a victim of monomania. I don't think he even heard what I said about Ralph Light. He jeered.

"Intuition! Our Irish lass has intuition. But now, Brigid Donovan, be good and give over pretending to be a detective. There's a good girl. Leave this to Ed. I intend to get him. I intend to get them both. He and his good-for-nothing mother."

I was sorry Ed felt the way he did about Jackie and Sid. But I could understand it. He had said one thing that tended to confirm my own views about Angele and her family. Her crimes were real and manifold. But she had also been badly used, as sinned against as sinning.

When I left Ed's, I went on to Edith's. "I want you to tell me more about Claire Du Lac," I told her.

"What's to tell? I've told you all there is to know. They were young, nineteen maybe, when they came down from Quebec. I think the move was her idea. She pretty much ran the family. She's an organizer. Always was."

Edith knits when she talks. She usually knits and looks you in the eye. Except when she's uneasy about something. Then, I've noticed, her needles seem to need all her attention. They suddenly seemed to need her attention.

I said, "There's something you're not telling me."

She said, "Oh?" It didn't sound innocent at all.

"Edith. Didn't it seem odd that the people the Du

221

Lacs worked for left them so much money? Was there any talk?"

She waved away the talk. "Talk!" she said. "There's always talk. What's talk? Hot air!"

"Yeah. You're right. But I want to know what it was people said. Tell me."

She sighed. It was a weary sound. "Just what you'd expect. They said she was being paid. It was all a payoff. All of it. Angele's marriage. The inheritance."

"A payoff for what?"

"Good God, Brigid, do I have to spell it out for you? They said she was old man Thorne's mistress."

"Thorne?"

"Yes. Thorne."

"Same family?"

"As David? Yes. He was their nephew I believe. An orphan or something. Anyway, they were like guardians."

"But you didn't believe the gossip. Why is that?"

"Well, for one thing, Claire Du Lac was the original Ice Maiden. Mind you, I wouldn't put anything past her. But I can't imagine her, couldn't imagine her, in bed with anyone. Not even her husband. Who would want to go to bed with her? No, Brigid, she wasn't nobody's mistress. I can just about guarantee that."

"So, the Thornes were just very generous."

"What else?"

Good question. And I thought I knew the answer. What I had to do next was get hold of Pat.

222

Chapter 22

I called Pat Monday at noon and got her. I was lucky. She was just on her way out.

"Have you seen Gen?" I asked.

"I did. I was just leaving for there. I followed Paul on — I guess it was Friday. Friday or Saturday. They're in a little brownstone. Not far from Emmaus. They have a summer sublet, furnished. The family that owns the house lives in what they call the garden apartment. They seem awfully nice people."

Having filled me in on these homely details, Pat lapsed into silence.

"Hello. Pat?"

"I'm here."

"I really wanted to know how she seems. Like, uh, who is she?"

"Well, she's not Jonathan. At least not when I've visited. It's hard to describe how she is. You know, Brigid, I've never thought of the two Gens as distinct personalities. St. Gen was always a little schizzy, and the other Gen, well, she was kind of like a mushroom growing in the dark. Like, without seeing her, I was still always aware of her presence? Something like that. It's like the two Gens are closer together now, nearer to being just one person. She's less schizzy and more open. She'll talk about the convent, and she's asked about Barney. But it's different. She's almost playful sometimes. But they say grace before meals, and I think she prays the rosary.

"She bought herself some cookbooks and she's learning how to cook. Something she never did in the convent. I've been over to dinner. Let's see. Chateaubriand. That was Saturday. That was good. Umh. Sunday we had boeuf bourguignon. That was excellent. She's making a quiche for lunch today. I should get over there."

I asked about her brother.

"Which one?"

"I meant Paul," I said.

She laughed. "Paul and Ralph are both her brothers. Remember? Paul is fine. He was wary of me when I first appeared on their doorstep. But when he realized I wasn't there to take Gen back, he relaxed. He is very fond of her. It's touching.

"And the other one, Ralph Light, he disappeared. They didn't hold him or even charge him. He insisted he was a friend of yours apparently. Said you'd given him the key. I think he was insinuating something about you, Brigid."

"About me?" I sensed her embarrassment across the miles of telephone wire. "What do you mean?"

"Oh, you know. That you'd invited him, he'd been there before with you. But then . . ." She faltered into silence again.

"But then, I had you with me instead?"

"Well!" It came out sounding huffy. "It's ridiculous. It was our being up there in your bed."

"You told them?"

"What was I supposed to do? They wanted to know where we were all that time."

I had difficulty not laughing. I said, "So he disappeared?"

"Yes he did. Along with about five thousand of Emmaus' money."

"Drug money?"

"I guess. Barney stopped payment on all of our checks."

"That was smart. So you'll get your road. How about the cloisters?" I said it to be mean.

"Oh, I hope so." And I don't think she was kidding.

"Pat. Do you think you could get Gen and Paul to fly up to Quebec City with you? Tomorrow. To visit Gram."

"I don't know. Maybe. Why?"

"I think I know what happened. I would like Paul up there to fill in some details. Also, from what you tell me, Gen is more comfortable with him around. And I want her there."

"Brigid! It's not Gen. Or Jonathan?"

225

"No. Neither of them."

She agreed to try to persuade them. She said she would call me at Edith's around three. To pass the time I drove to Alamoosook Lake and went swimming.

It was just three when she called back.

"No problem," she said. She sounded surprised.

I said, "She wanted me to bring Gen up there. I'll call her and tell her to expect us, Gen and me, say six or six-thirty? Shall we meet at the Frontenac?"

I called Gram. She was annoyed to find I was still in Maine. Hearing I would bring Gen to her the next evening mollified her. Some.

Next I called Bob Templeton. I told him my plan. He was less than enthusiastic. He said, "You're dealing with a murderer, Brigid. Remember?"

"Yeahbut, it doesn't have anything to do with the present. You know what I mean?"

"The murders happened in the present. I think you're being romantic."

He meant foolish, he was just being polite. He said, "What if I came along?"

The thought was comforting, but I hedged. "I can't arrive there in a police car."

"Well," he said, "we could go together in yours. Or better yet, I could go up in mine. That way no one would even know I was there."

To that I agreed.

It was dusk when I arrived at Nell's house. In the waning light, it looked abandoned, the grass ankle high, the dandelions no longer a pretty yellow, but long stemmed and topped with dingy seed balls. The garden looked like we were growing weeds this year and the peas were a mess. Inside it smelled musty. Too late, I regretted my decision to come home.

In the kitchen I fried a clove of garlic in some olive oil which helped the odor. Then I popped some corn and curled up on the couch with my pillow and an afghan and watched Cagney and Lacey. I didn't know Lacey had a drinking problem. I don't watch TV much.

Chapter 23

It was still twilight when I woke. There was no hope of sleeping anymore, not that my sleep had been refreshing. It hadn't, for I had dreamed all night of my coming confrontation with the old woman. Nothing straightforward. But, awake, I could read all my anxieties in the images of the night: a humongous yard sale, like the ones all up and down Route One in summer, this one in front of a mansion like Norumbega in Camden.

I loathe yard sales but Pat, or some elusive presence I think was Pat, maybe it was all the Pats,

228

all the elusive loves I have ever known, she insisted we stop. On every table something of mine was for sale. Around back I saw my car; on the porch, my children in a kind of bird cage. Jackie was for sale, so was Gen. I tried to buy them all, though I knew my pockets were empty.

It turned out to be an auction. No matter how high I bid, Gram bid higher. "Five hundred dollars," she would say, and then add, "That's American." The auctioneer would never recognize my last bid and he knocked each item down to her. Jackie got sold to her three times that way.

The bidding for Angele woke me, sweating with tension. I got up and went out to the garden to weed the peas. There were thousands of slugs on everything.

Bob called around eight to say he was starting out. "Don't even think about me," he said. "But I'll be there. If there's any trouble, smash a window or something."

"Right. I don't think there'll be trouble."

"Well. I guess. Brigid, if your instinct tells you it's dangerous, for God's sake, lay off. Promise me."

"I hear you. I won't push it."

I tried to absorb my nervous tension by laboring. I succeeded in exhausting myself, but I was still on edge, even after hoeing, mowing, and vacuuming. But the place looked like home again when I was done. I made up the other guest room for Sid. I picked what strawberries the birds had overlooked and made a shortcake from Bisquick. For our coming-home treat.

I left shortly after noon and got to Quebec City by five. I parked in the lot just inside the wall, thinking the walk down the Rue St. Louis would

229

settle my nerves, but the mindless gaiety of the maddening crowd only made me irritable.

I was early, but the three of them were out pacing the sidewalk alongside the Frontenac. Only Gen was happy. Happy to see me, happy to be in Quebec City, happy to be going to Grandmother's house.

Paul seemed distant, as he had the other time I met him, but courteous and protective of Genevieve.

Pat looked beautiful, beautiful and worried. She wore a dress of pale blue butcher's linen, the gored skirt falling in soft folds around the calves of her legs, the bodice fitted, with wide lapels. Her shoes had a modest heel and a demure strap. Altogether a million-dollar look of sophistication. Her burnished hair was like the shining helmet of an ancient goddess of war and wisdom. Athena perhaps. The look of her reassured me; she intended to see us through.

I wished I had had an opportunity to consult with her. I wished I had something else to wear. A tuxedo maybe, and patent leather pumps; but my shoes were almost new and the holes over my little toes were still very small, almost imperceptible I thought.

Gen and Paul walked ahead, Gen chattering.

I said to Pat, "She seems happy."

"She has been. I hope she can continue to be. What's going to happen?"

"God knows. You should probably know before we get there that Gram wanted Gen's typewriter to forge a letter from Gen accusing you of seduction."

"Good Lord!"

"Oh, that's the good news. The date on the letter is two days after Gen left Surry, so it clearly is a forgery. The bad news is that Gram sent copies of it to the Diocesan office in Maine and another one to your Mother House in New Hampshire."

Pat waved my bad news aside. "They think she's crazy," she said. "It doesn't matter. Not really." Then she asked, "What are you planning to do with us at Gram's?"

"I wish we had time to talk. I'm going to rake over some past history. Please support me."

She laughed. "That sounds mighty like 'trust me.' "

Marie opened the door for us. Gram was seated in her usual place. Jesus from the mantel surveyed the scene with calm disinterest, diffident even about his bleeding heart which he seemed about to hide with his hand. Gen greeted her grandmother lovingly with a kiss; Paul was more formal. Gram had Gen draw up a chair and sit close beside her. I managed to claim my old seat by the anemones. A table light made the enamel petals glow.

Gram said, "Six o'clock is a strange time for a visit. I do not expect you Paul. I have Marie make us a big tea." She totally ignored Pat who sat on a bench near the window, like a recording angel, not a participant at all. A beam of late afternoon sun caught her hair. She reminded me of a Fra Angelico, bright and glittery in the gloomy room. I wished I had thought to tell her to smash the window if things got rough.

Tea was elaborate and I realized that I had not eaten all day. I helped myself to cantaloupe and sliced ham. I gestured with my plate to Pat, but she shook her head no.

The sounds of our eating grew loud in an uncomfortable silence until Gram said, "Genevieve, I am very glad you come here to stay with me, your grand-mère. It is time."

Gen looked alarmed. Paul said, "She's not staying, Gram. She and I have an apartment now in New York. We work as volunteers at a place called Emmaus."

Gram looked to me as if for an explanation. I don't know why. All she had asked me to do was deliver the goods. And I had. But she was right: The time for explanations had come. I thought most of them, however, would come from her.

I put my empty plate on the table and began.

"Mrs. Du Lac, I think our present troubles began a long time ago. A long time ago. I think they started when Angele was a child, when you and your husband first got that job at the Thorne's. How old was Angele then?"

"Five. She is five. But I do not understand you. We have no troubles now. And this is something I do not wish to speak on."

"Well, Mrs. Du Lac, I guess I think you're wrong. I think we do still have troubles. And they need talking about."

I had committed *lèse majesté* and everyone knew it. Gen gasped. Gram looked haughty and she looked mad.

I rushed on. "I think it was Angele who got you that job at Thorne's."

"Why! This is stupid! She is five. I get that job."

"You accepted the offer, certainly. But it was Angele he was buying. I'm willing to believe you might not have known, not at first perhaps. You maybe couldn't imagine in the beginning why he offered the job to you. Your husband was in the Allagash that first winter when you went out there to live. Wasn't he? Did you live with the Thornes in the big house that first winter?"

She didn't say a thing. She no longer even tried to stop me. The palms of my hands were wet, I guess from fear. But I was gathering strength from my own voice.

"Did Angele ever tell you, or try to tell you, what was happening to her? Did you tell her that was love? Did you tell her that Mr. Thorne loved her? Did you tell her to be a good girl and do what he said? What did you say to her? How did you manage to control her?"

My taunting, meant to break down the old lady, broke Gen instead. In the voice of the saint, Genevieve said, "Miss Donóvan, you mustn't talk that way to Grand-mère. And you mustn't say those things about my mother. My mother was a very very good woman."

Tears had started to roll down her cheeks. "My mother would never do anything wrong like what you're saying."

I used her interruption. I asked, "What am I saying, Gen? What am I saying she did wrong?"

Gen hesitated, reluctant to name the scandal, her face haggard as she stammered, "You're saying she let Mr. Thorne do those nasty things to her."

"What nasty things?"

"Those nasty things! Love!" Her eyes opened wide in astonishment, confounded by a paradox that was insoluble, one her mind, unable to comprehend, forever ran from.

"How can love be nasty?" I asked, spelling it out. "Did your mother tell you to do things that she called love?"

Bewildered, St. Gen nodded. She said, "We always loved her. Every afternoon we loved her. We were good." It sounded like a question, one she had been asking all her life. Hoping all her life for an answer she never expected to hear. I gave it to her, for what it was worth.

"Of course you were good. You did what your mother told you to. That was good."

For a moment she looked relieved. But for a moment only. She began to nod, and then she changed. Her face, her body, everything was altered but in a way too subtle to define. There was a new hardness in the muscles of her mouth, a coolness in her eyes. She said, and her voice had lost its breathless sweetness, "We were very bad. We did very bad things to her. We were wicked children. She tried to make us better. She beat us just as hard as she could, so it wasn't her fault we were so bad. But it was never any use at all. We would never be good children. Every day, every day. Bad, bad, bad.

"She even put our heads under water to make the bad go away. She burned our feet to make it go. Fire and water. Water and fire. But we had the devil in us, hiding in us and she couldn't make him leave. He wouldn't go. He wouldn't go. He wouldn't go."

A crafty look overtook her eyes, hiding them. She turned to gram. She said, "You knew it too, you fucking bitch. Didn't you?"

Gram's face contracted in pain. Gen laughed. Or was it Gen? Paul rose and went to her. "Jon," he said. "Old buddy. You want to go home?"

234

"No I don't want to go home! Mind your own fucking business. Go sit down. I want to hear what else this lady has to say." She gestured toward me.

"Well, I do not," said Mrs. Du Lac. "I hear quite enough. I want you to leave this house immediately." She shook her finger at me.

"Go on. Don't pay any attention to her. This is fun." It was Jon speaking.

I had no intention of seriously crossing Jonathan. Even Paul had gone back to his chair with a resigned sigh. I think he had decided that if I knew the truth, the truth should out. The sore had festered long enough. Had festered in the dark, known but unnamed. It was time to name it, to lance it, to let the poison drain.

I said, "Angele was sexually abused when she was a child, that's pretty clear. There's her abuse of her own children. And her precocious sexuality. I don't imagine, Mrs. Du Lac, you let her play much with other children, not after Pat. You must have been terrified your secret would be found out.

"From what I've heard about you, Mrs. Du Lac, and about your husband, I doubted it was either of you who were molesting her. So, it seemed obvious it had to have been the generous Mr. Thorne."

"Lies," she said contemptuously.

"No," I said, "not lies. Maybe for the first time it's the truth. You have always thought you knew better, knew best. I have tried to imagine how you could ever had allowed these things to happen to Angele. What I believe is, you actually encouraged it."

"You believe this. You believe that. Who cares what you believe. You have a dirty mind. That is what I believe." But she said it without conviction, from force of habit. "These things you talk about, they never happen."

"Yeah. They did. I think all of you blamed Angele. She was the family scapegoat. Angele was the seducer. When she seduced her own children, she was only fulfilling the role you cast for her from the beginning."

"It was that one," she pointed toward the window. It was her first acknowledgment of Pat's presence. "There is the one who seduces innocent children. She is the one who corrupts my Angele."

"Fucking A!" Jonathan threw in.

"You know, Mrs. Du Lac," I said, "that just isn't so. "You sold your daughter, Mrs. Du Lac."

I let the silence grow a while before I continued. "You acquired a small fortune and you provided for her by marrying her off to a dependent of the old man. Did David Thorne have money of his own, or did his inheritance depend on following his uncle's orders and marrying Angele?"

Gram had been communing silently with Jesus over the mantel, acting as though what I had to say was inconsequential and boring. But she couldn't resist an opportunity at David bashing. She said, "When they marry, he has nothing. Only his uncle's good will. He is nothing without my Angele. But later, then he inherits money. No one expects it."

"So everyone gets rich but Angele. Angele gets her allowance if she's a good girl. What happened, Mrs. Du Lac, when Angele was bad? Was she ever bad? Did she ever make old Mr. Thorne angry?"

"She is always a willful little girl. A willful woman. She is a drunk."

"What would you do? Would you jerk her

236

allowance when she was bad? When she stood up for herself? Did you threaten her with poverty? Did you make that sound like hell?"

She looked surprised. "It's true. We are poor people. Angele, she never seems to understand this."

"Well, that must have been terrible, that Angele didn't understand what was really at stake." But my sarcasm was lost on her. "So Angele grows up and is married off to David. Who controlled the money then? You? David?"

She snorted. "David is nothing. He is nothing, only a drunk. Both of them, nothing but drunks. I manage their money. Until he inherits!" She was clearly disgusted, no doubt at fate.

I asked, "When David inherited his money, did he take over control of Angele? Did he become the one who controlled her allowance?"

"Of course. She is nothing but a drunk. No one can control her."

I realized that in Mrs. Du Lac's eyes all of us were nothing buts. I said, "Lately he had been giving his money away." She rolled back her eyes and made the sign of the cross. "Had any separate provision been made for Angele, or was she completely dependent on David and his good will?"

Gram looked puzzled. I said, "I'm asking whether Angele could be threatened with poverty the way she was threatened as a child. When David began to give his money away, was Angele afraid she might end up poor?"

Gram pushed aside some air, or maybe it was Angele she pushed aside. "Her! Who knows what she thinks?"

"Well, what are the facts? What arrangements did

you make with Mr. Thorne? Did Angele have money under her own control?"

"Her own control?" The old lady echoed me as if I were mad and my words evidence. "Of course not. She is married to David."

"What if he had left her?"

"He cannot. He lose his money."

"The money his uncle left him. But what about his own inheritance?"

With another wave of her hand, she dismissed David's inheritance. I asked, "Did David inherit before Paul was born or after?"

"Much after. Maybe five years, six years."

"Right before his disappearance in fact."

"Yes."

"Mrs. Du Lac, I think you know that Angele murdered her husband. That she was drunk, did it in a blackout, but did it because she had been goaded beyond endurance by his giving away money. She saw looming that hell you always threatened her with. She thought he was making her a pauper."

Gram interrupted. "It was that bastard Sid." But again, it was without conviction, just lines in the play. She said, "The little bastard comes to his papa for more money."

"You've got the wrong bastard, Mrs. Du Lac. It wasn't Sid who came that night. That night it was Ralph Light who came for more money. That as the bastard Angele spoke of. Not Sid."

I waited for some response, but none came. The silence convinced me that I was right: both Paul and his grandmother had known all along that Ralph Light had visited David Thorne the night he was killed. That's all I needed to be sure that I was correct in my interpretation of what had happened afterwards.

"Ralph Light knew that David and Angele were to have dinner together early in the evening, before his own appointment with David. When he got there the evidence of Angele's presence was everywhere. I believe he went out and called you, Mrs. Du Lac. What I think happened is this. Ralph Light discovered David's body. His first thought was there wasn't going to be any more free money from Papa. He realized that it was Angele who had done it. So he called you with a proposition. I think what he suggested was something like this, that he would clean up all the evidence that Angele had been there, and in return you would pay him something for his trouble.

"I think you agreed to his proposal. I think you agreed because you figured he was at least as vulnerable as Angele, perhaps more vulnerable. I think you figured when he asked for his money, you'd tell him to get lost or you'd call the cops.

"Then Ed called. He must have arrived at the cottage right after Ralph left it. Ed didn't waste any time. He cleaned up any trace of Angele and then went to call you. What he told you was that Sid had killed David. He really believed that. He knew nothing about Ralph Light. When Angele told him David was going to see his bastard that night, Ed thought she meant Sid.

"Of course, Ed had played right into your hands. And you've been playing it that way ever since. Blaming Sid for something you knew Angele had done."

The room had become very still. Everyone was

listening. Jesus, his head, cocked at an angle, listened, the pointing finger of his left hand raised now for silence.

I learned my first summer at camp, some four decades ago, that it is always safe to blame someone who isn't there. I had blamed Angele for her husband's murder. She might not have been everyone's favorite choice, but as her condition of not being among us was permanent, no one objected. To account for her murder, however, I was going to run into the difficulty of naming one among us. I wiped my palms on my thighs. My palms were wet, but my throat was dry.

"You agreed, Mrs. Du Lac, to provide Angele with an alibi, and Ed brought her up here that night. He was determined to marry her in order to protect that alibi. And he suggested to you that it wouldn't hurt to hire me to investigate the murder. He pointed out that my landlady was Sid's aunt. That way I'd be close to Sid's family. When I uncovered Sid's connection to David Thorne and saw in that a motive for murder, it would have a great deal more weight than if you or he brought it to the attention of the police.

"But you had your own scheme for me. I don't think you much cared about what happened to Angele. What you did care about was protecting the good name of your family. It wouldn't suit the image of yourself here on Parc des Gouverneurs all the stuff Angele might reveal. And you were very afraid that if she was questioned by the police, held in custody without a drink, she might say almost anything. She might even begin to tell the truth. After all, she was nothing but a drunk.

"So you agreed to hire me, but what you wanted from me was a typewriter. The typewriter Genevieve used when she wrote to you. You wanted it to forge a letter which would ruin Sr. Pat and destroy the convent. Which would absolve you of any blame for the abuse, the abuse you were responsible for."

The old lady had covered her ears. It was a weary gesture. Her head bent under a weight too immense for her fragile neck to bear. She seemed diminished. She said, "Lies. All lies." But the worst was still to come."

"You called your grandson Paul at Emmaus."

"I never did!" She raised her head, the spark in her eye reminiscent of old times, of her old self. I got that one wrong.

"No, she didn't call me," Paul intervened. "I simply came up after Father's funeral."

"Be still, Paul. She knows nothing. Guesses. Bad guesses."

"No, Grand-mère. She knows. And she is right. It is best now that everyone knows."

"Paul, don't! Please don't." It was Gen speaking. Not St. Genevieve. Not Jonathan.

"Gen. It will be all right. And it's best." He turned back to me. "Miss Donovan, my grandmother told me what Angele had done. You see, my father was very important to me. He . . . He . . . He showed me how to live."

Paul was having trouble maintaining control. His voice rolled jerkily over half-buried sobs. "I think he showed both of us. Gen and me. I know what he did to Gen. For years I hated him. But when he came back, he was so changed. I was sixteen and he . . . and he . . ."

241

He cried quietly for a moment before he pulled himself together. "I'm sorry. He helped me find myself. He helped me find my higher power. Gen too."

I remembered what Gen had said that first time we met, that David's death had been a sacrifice by which some wretched soul might be saved. Had she known then in some intuitive way that her brother Paul was that soul?

Paul continued, "When Gram told me what Angele had done, I don't know. I, I . . . I went and killed her."

"Oh, Paul! No, no, no, no!" Gen rose and threw herself at her brother, toppling him and the chair onto the floor. Pat left her place by the window and rushed toward them. The front bell rang and someone started pounding on the heavy door. Marie's scream sounded shrill from the hallway.

Gram and I alone were motionless, our eyes locked in a separate dimension. It was as if we were God's first creations formed out of chaos: still, clear and intelligent. I said, "What did you say to him, Mrs. Du Lac, to have him commit murder for you?"

Her eyes blinked once.

"Did you remind him of all she had put him through? Put Gen through? Did you admit to knowing all that?"

She blinked again. She said, "I tell him a man avenges his father's murder. I remind him of Orestes."

"But David Thorne wasn't his father."

I caught a flicker of surprise in the cold depths of her eyes. For once I had been a step ahead of her.

She had a comeback, but it was late, and it was

lame. She said, "Humph! Not his father. Quel imagination!"

Bob Templeton's voice overrode the riot in the room behind us. "Brigid! What's going on? Are you all right?"

Before I turned, I glanced up at Jesus. His heart peeped coyly through his fingers at me, but his downcast eyes, big and sad, refused to meet my own.

"Yeah," I said. "I'm all right. Can we get out of here?"

Chapter 24

I spent the night at the Chateau Frontenac, and
I've never regretted it.

Bob took Paul into informal custody right there at
the house on Parc des Gouverneurs. He offered to
take Gen and Pat along as far as Jackman. They
called before they left to arrange for the Thorne
lawyer to meet them at the border.

It was a subdued parting. I told Pat I'd come to
see her in a day or two.

I drew her aside. We stood at the window. It had

begun to rain. I said, "Keep Paul from admitting anything. Don't let him talk about it."

Pat looked at me, indulgently.

"Okay. So I didn't have to tell you that. The thing is," I said, "Bob would rather not know. No one in Greenville will thank him for arresting a kid who's been through what Paul's been through. And Bob has to live the rest of his life in Greenville. With his mother. And his grandmother. And Nell. And probably with Jackie Soper and Sid."

Gram had withdrawn from the scene in her parlor when Bob rushed in. So we never had a chance to say goodbye.

It took me another month to wind up my history of H.O.P.E. I sent it to Gram. She never acknowledged it. I wasn't surprised. But I sent it registered, so I know she received it. Then a few months later I got a package in the mail from Edith. It was a copy of the history printed. In her note, Edith invited me to dinner.

Jackie bought a trailer. It sits behind the house near the dock there at Nell's in Greenville. They include me in all their plans. The trailer is one of those with a bow window at the end. Sid didn't stay. "Too many weird people," he muttered. He was looking at me. He's back down at H.O.P.E. But he's got his own car now and he comes to visit his mother and his aunt, and, when I'm not there, he stays over.

Gen entered counseling, and in January she enrolled as a student at the College of the Atlantic in Bar Harbor. Pat sees her just about every weekend and is full of hope for her, and for Paul as well.

Paul was never charged with anything. The

murders, officially at least, were never solved. Paul, too, began intensive counseling, and he began to work as a literacy volunteer at the prison in Thomaston. It was like doing time, but in his own way. He took to living at the convent in an out-building he put up with Sid's help. In the spring, the two of them, Sid and Paul, began work on the cloisters.

I still Twelfth Step Ed whenever I'm in town, visiting Pat or visiting Edith and my favorite Holstein, Beatrice.

A few of the publications of
THE NAIAD PRESS, INC.
P.O. Box 10543 ● Tallahassee, Florida 32302
Phone (904) 539-5965
Mail orders welcome. Please include 15% postage.

MURDER IS RELATIVE by Karen Saum. 256 pp. The first
Brigid Donovan mystery. ISBN 0-941483-70-3 $8.95

A ROOM FULL OF WOMEN by Elisabeth Nonas. 256 pp.
Contemporary Lesbian lives. ISBN 0-941483-69-X 8.95

PRIORITIES by Lynda Lyons 288 pp. Science fiction with a
twist. ISBN 0-941483-66-5 8.95

THEME FOR DIVERSE INSTRUMENTS by Jane Rule.
208 pp. Powerful romantic lesbian stories. ISBN 0-941483-63-0 8.95

LESBIAN QUERIES by Hertz & Ertman. 112 pp. The questions
you were too embarrassed to ask. ISBN 0-941483-67-3 8.95

CLUB 12 by Amanda Kyle Williams. 288 pp. Espionage thriller
featuring a lesbian agent! ISBN 0-941483-64-9 8.95

DEATH DOWN UNDER by Claire McNab. 240 pp. 3rd Det.
Insp. Carol Ashton mystery. ISBN 0-941483-39-8 8.95

MONTANA FEATHERS by Penny Hayes. 256 pp. Vivian and
Elizabeth find love in frontier Montana. ISBN 0-941483-61-4 8.95

CHESAPEAKE PROJECT by Phyllis Horn. 304 pp. Jessie &
Meredith in perilous adventure. ISBN 0-941483-58-4 8.95

LIFESTYLES by Jackie Calhoun. 224 pp. Contemporary Lesbian
lives and loves. ISBN 0-941483-57-6 8.95

VIRAGO by Karen Marie Christa Minns. 208 pp. Darsen has
chosen Ginny. ISBN 0-941483-56-8 8.95

WILDERNESS TREK by Dorothy Tell. 192 pp. Six women on
vacation learning "new" skills. ISBN 0-941483-60-6 8.95

MURDER BY THE BOOK by Pat Welch. 256 pp. A Helen
Black Mystery. First in a series. ISBN 0-941483-59-2 8.95

BERRIGAN by Vicki P. McConnell. 176 pp. Youthful Lesbian–
romantic, idealistic Berrigan. ISBN 0-941483-55-X 8.95

LESBIANS IN GERMANY by Lillian Faderman & B. Eriksson.
128 pp. Fiction, poetry, essays. ISBN 0-941483-62-2 8.95

THE BEVERLY MALIBU by Katherine V. Forrest. 288 pp. A
Kate Delafield Mystery. 3rd in a series. ISBN 0-941483-47-9 16.95

THERE'S SOMETHING I'VE BEEN MEANING TO TELL
YOU Ed. by Loralee MacPike. 288 pp. Gay men and lesbians
coming out to their children. ISBN 0-941483-44-4 9.95
ISBN 0-941483-54-1 16.95

WOMAN PLUS WOMAN by Dolores Klaich. 300 pp. Supurb
Lesbian overview.   ISBN 0-941483-28-2   9.95

SLOW DANCING AT MISS POLLY'S by Sheila Ortiz Taylor.
96 pp. Lesbian Poetry   ISBN 0-941483-30-4   7.95

DOUBLE DAUGHTER by Vicki P. McConnell. 216 pp. A Nyla
Wade Mystery, third in the series.   ISBN 0-941483-26-6   8.95

HEAVY GILT by Delores Klaich. 192 pp. Lesbian detective/
disappearing homophobes/upper class gay society.
                                      ISBN 0-941483-25-8   8.95

THE FINER GRAIN by Denise Ohio. 216 pp. Brilliant young
college lesbian novel.   ISBN 0-941483-11-8   8.95

THE AMAZON TRAIL by Lee Lynch. 216 pp. Life, travel & lore
of famous lesbian author.   ISBN 0-941483-27-4   8.95

HIGH CONTRAST by Jessie Lattimore. 264 pp. Women of the
Crystal Palace.   ISBN 0-941483-17-7   8.95

OCTOBER OBSESSION by Meredith More. Josie's rich, secret
Lesbian life.   ISBN 0-941483-18-5   8.95

LESBIAN CROSSROADS by Ruth Baetz. 276 pp. Contemporary
Lesbian lives.   ISBN 0-941483-21-5   9.95

BEFORE STONEWALL: THE MAKING OF A GAY AND
LESBIAN COMMUNITY by Andrea Weiss & Greta Schiller.
96 pp., 25 illus.   ISBN 0-941483-20-7   7.95

WE WALK THE BACK OF THE TIGER by Patricia A. Murphy.
192 pp. Romantic Lesbian novel/beginning women's movement.
                                      ISBN 0-941483-13-4   8.95

SUNDAY'S CHILD by Joyce Bright. 216 pp. Lesbian athletics, at
last the novel about sports.   ISBN 0-941483-12-6   8.95

OSTEN'S BAY by Zenobia N. Vole. 204 pp. Sizzling adventure
romance set on Bonaire.   ISBN 0-941483-15-0   8.95

LESSONS IN MURDER by Claire McNab. 216 pp. 1st Det. Inspec.
Carol Ashton mystery — erotic tension!.   ISBN 0-941483-14-2   8.95

YELLOWTHROAT by Penny Hayes. 240 pp. Margarita, bandit,
kidnaps Julia.   ISBN 0-941483-10-X   8.95

SAPPHISTRY: THE BOOK OF LESBIAN SEXUALITY by
Pat Califia. 3d edition, revised. 208 pp.   ISBN 0-941483-24-X   8.95

CHERISHED LOVE by Evelyn Kennedy. 192 pp. Erotic
Lesbian love story.   ISBN 0-941483-08-8   8.95

LAST SEPTEMBER by Helen R. Hull. 208 pp. Six stories & a
glorious novella.   ISBN 0-941483-09-6   8.95

THE SECRET IN THE BIRD by Camarin Grae. 312 pp. Striking,
psychological suspense novel.   ISBN 0-941483-05-3   8.95